UNIVERSE 6

Universe 6

EDITED BY TERRY CARR

Doubleday & Company, Inc.
GARDEN CITY, NEW YORK, 1976

DESIGNED BY LAURENCE ALEXANDER

ISBN: 0-385-11413-3
Library of Congress Catalog Card Number 75–21216
"The Wine Has Been Left Open Too Long and the
Memory Has Gone Flat" by Harlan Ellison. Copy-
right © 1976 by Harlan Ellison. Appears with
permission of the Author and the Author's agent,
Robert P. Mills, Ltd., New York, N.Y.
Copyright © 1976 by Terry Carr

CONTENTS

BRIAN ALDISS, *whose novels include* Greybeard *and* Frankenstein Unbound, *is one of the most important science fiction writers of the past decade—not only because of his great talent, but because he has continued to explore new fictional territory year after year.*

Here, in his first story for Universe, *he tells an absorbing tale of research into human consciousness, of the discovery that different time-flows run concurrently in the brain. It sounds like a terribly serious, significant story, and it is . . . but Aldiss makes of it something more, a wry, even playful commentary on people.*

Journey to the Heartland

BY BRIAN W. ALDISS

At certain times of day the campus was full of people. Students and college professors alike paraded in the sunshine, talking, calling, flirting, reading—a bright flock almost as migratory as birds. Five minutes later, they would all be gone to classroom or playing field or canteen, leaving the area deserted.

The windows of the Dream Research Unit looked down on the parade. Andrew Angsteed looked down through the windows. He was head of the unit. He was tall, casually dressed; his hair was graying. People found him remote. The hubbub from below rose to his ears. On the whole, he preferred the campus empty.

Behind him, in the laboratory, his three assistants worked, transcribing and codifying the previous night's work. Angsteed walked past the row of caged cats with their shaven heads. A thin beam of sun, slanting in the end window, lit the last cage; its occupant rolled over on her back, purring as

Angsteed passed. He went to the window and drew down the blind.

Then he retreated into his office and put his head between his hands.

Rose-Jean Dempson was awakened by the yellow buzzer.

She opened her eyes. The scene that drifted in on her senses was without meaning, an affair of walls, angles, and corners in which she was not remotely interested, so vivid remained the perspectives in which she had just been moving namelessly.

Moving carefully so as not to detach electrodes, she pulled herself onto one elbow and reached for a microphone by the bedside.

"4:17. I dreamed I was on a train in the Jurassic Age. It was a funny train, all full of beautiful furry surfaces. They were like big moths. I don't think they were alive. I wasn't scared of them. It didn't seem to be Jurassic time outside, at least not at first.

"My husband was in the dream. We had been to a party with a lot of people. Maybe it was somewhere under ground. I had left without him to catch the train. Yet he was also on the train. That sounds confusing, but it wasn't in the dream. He was at the party and he was also on the train. I kept wondering how I could save him. I loved him best in the world and I wanted to be perfectly possessed by him; but he would not come all the way toward me. That was why I was having to go into the Jurassic, I think.

"Someone was arguing with me. It was a ticket collector. He was old and gray but very solid, very fatherly. He did not seem to see my husband. He was telling me to get off the train.

"I said, 'There are things which have never been done before. I have to tell my husband to let go of his strict self-control. He has to reject all the things he thinks he loves, or else he will die. He must be more random, as these moths appear to be.'

"But I knew that was wrong, somehow. The ticket collector would not let me explain properly. He shook his head and said something like, 'The essence of human life can only be a matter of cyclic repetition.'

"I was trying to explain to people that my madness, my wish to roam, was a special, life-giving quality. My husband had to admire, accept, and emulate it. I knew this meant suffering for him, but only in that way could he make his inner life flower. Everything else in the compartment was flowering, the upholstery and everything, but he sat there almost like a pile of luggage. I must have identified with him in some way, because I also felt like a thing all of a sudden.

"There were strange lumpy people moving along the corridor of the train.

"When I lay down on the seat, I realized it was night outside. We were gliding through the outer suburbs of a huge city. The train was a blaze of flame and foliage and bright things. Just above the rim of the window, I saw cold lights that fled by in the dark—white, white, white, white, white, repetitive, chilled nine hundred times. Very threatening. They were lighting wide deserted roads. Then there were dark houses. Then spots of sodium lighting, threaded out thin. Then country. Blackness.

"A different blackness from my blackness. Mine was rich and warm, personal, unregulated. The outer darkness had been chilled by the little urban lights. I tried to explain to my husband that the mad and the sane met here, that the lights were the lights of the sane—in those two camps of the world, the sane were winning by sheer force of numbers, pushing their cold little nonradiant lights out into the countryside.

"There was a terrific noise as we went over a bridge. I was excited because I thought we were getting near the Jurassic. The moths were very thick and bright.

"Then the bell rang."

Rose-Jean looked about the laboratory, thick with mute noises of machines. Then she settled her dark head down on the pillow and fell asleep. Ninety-two minutes later, the yellow buzzer roused her again.

Andrew Angsteed and Rose-Jean Dempson walked back from town. The sun was low, casting long poplar shadows across the fields toward the university, where a few windows were already lit against dusk.

"I'm going to be away next week," Angsteed said. "Or did I already tell you that? Do you want a break from work, Rose-Jean?"

"No, I'm not tired at all. Besides, I'm off duty tonight."

"But you've been on nights for six weeks now, going on seven."

"I can't exactly explain, Andrew, but I'm refreshed by my dreams. Since you've been recording them, they have become much more vivid. I feel as if—as if a whole new side of my personality was coming into being."

A silence between them. Before it could grow too long and awkward, Angsteed said, "You've become my star guinea pig, Rose-Jean. As you know, our interest on the project is simply to categorize, not analyze, dreams. We've identified three main types, or think we have—sigma, tau, and ypsilon, and over a five-year period we are specializing in the tau-type, which is a phenomenon of median second-quarter sleep. In other words, we are concerned with classification, not with the dream content *per se*. What is beginning to emerge is that the tau-type is a more multilayered dream than the other kinds. But your dreams—your tau dreams, Rose-Jean . . . well, I happen to find them extraordinarily beautiful, interesting, and significant. I mean nothing personal—"

She looked up at his face and said, "Dreams aren't exactly personal, are they?"

"No, let me finish! Just because I'm in charge of the project, I may seem remote at times. You know that our findings are being challenged by Dr. Rudesci in St. Louis." He paused. "Have I said this to you before?"

"No. Well—yes, in a way. Sometimes. People have been

known to repeat themselves, Andrew, especially if it is something that is worrying them."

They had come to the gate into New Buildings. He paused and took her hand.

"Don't let's go in yet! I have to talk to you. Rose-Jean, I have fallen completely for you. You must have noticed. You're so beautiful and your dreams are so beautiful. I've never been so close to anyone's inner world. . . ."

She looked searchingly at him, so that he could devour once again the sight of that perfect conjunction between nose, nostrils, upper lip, and mouth, and the unique placement of her eyes, eyes that he had so often surreptitiously gazed on when, closed and inward-gazing, they were merely the most entrancing part of his research project.

"You'd better come up and have coffee in my room, Andrew," she said.

Hers was the ordinary untidy room of a young faculty teacher. He noted books on her shelves that one might find in any of twenty adjacent rooms: Tilbane's *Lord of the Rocks; The Grand Claim of Being; Sex in Theory and Practice;* Orlick's *After the Post-Renaissance;* his own *Sense and the Dreaming Self; What I Know About Mars;* Loupescu on Time; Krawstadt's *Frankenstein Among the Arts;* and others. There were also drawings and gouache paintings scattered about.

By the window was a framed photograph of her with a man, laughing.

He picked up one of the gouaches. It showed a girl sitting decorously nude against a panther. "Did you do this?" he asked. The colors were crude.

"Please. It's not finished. Besides, it isn't very good."

He watched her push her paintings away in a locker. She was right, that must be admitted; the painting wasn't very good; her dreams were much more striking.

Straightening, she said, "I keep painting the same picture

over and over again, as if that one image is all I have to offer, I don't know why. It's as if my essence was just repetitive."

"The essence of human life can only be a matter of cyclic repetition, since all generations are similar, have similar archetypal experiences."

"I meant repetitive within myself. Maybe all my dreams would boil down to repetition, if they were analyzed."

He suspected she was trying for pathos. He replied with a great effort at warmth, "I would not think that at all. There are always certain recurrent archetypes in dreams, but much of the other content of your dreams I find highly original and thought-provoking."

"Is that really so? What sort of things—I mean, may I ask—?"

"Take your last dream, the one about traveling by train into the Jurassic. I've played your report over several times. I found it interesting the way you contrasted the mad and the cold sane. Your sympathies were with the mad. You evidently see our urban culture, nominally built by the sane, as a sinister thing—a threat to *true* sanity, which is allied to madness."

She put her hand over her mouth. "Do I really? Did I say that? Oh, it sounds very profound. . . . My subject's really domestic science. . . . Maybe I should get us some coffee, would you like that?"

"The dream world—right at its heartland lies an extraordinary amalgam of sanity and madness. . . ." His attempt at explanation hung in the silence of her banal room.

He watched her preparing coffee, dearly wishing that she would offer him whiskey. He recalled that she did not touch alcohol. Perhaps he could change that, given time.

She looked so cool, so lovely, in her simple outfit of slacks, blouse, and suede waistcoat. He went over to her and put an arm around her.

"Rose-Jean, the work has taken on new meaning for me since you joined our unit as a volunteer." As he said the words he thought how pedestrian they sounded. The language of dreams was so much more eloquent than the poor, defaced coinage of waking.

She took the opportunity to ask, "What do you hope to find out from these researches? You must believe in them—you've dedicated so much time to them."

"There are things that have never been done. Haven't I said this to you before? It's some while since it was discovered that there were different kinds of sleep. Now we are sure that there are different kinds of dreams—although the situation looks more complex than when I launched the project, nine years ago. I think at last I have the answer. . . ."

"And what's that? What sort of answer?"

"Oh, forget it. Let's not talk shop. Rose-Jean!" He grasped her and tried to kiss her. She struggled in his arms but he would not let her go. She submitted, bringing her lips to his. Although she stood unyieldingly, after a second she parted her lips slightly, so that he could taste the warmth rising from within her, the furnace of her. He cupped her left breast with one hand before letting her go.

She retreated, hand up to mouth again.

"Andrew, I'm not psychologically prepared for this kind of assault!"

" 'Assault'!"

"As you may know, I'm living separate from my husband, but he is still around and—I may as well tell you this—he still occupies much of my thoughts. Now, please let me pour you some coffee."

He clutched his head. "As I say—the essence of human life is cyclic—archetypal emotions, sensations, experiences. They don't change. . . . Sometimes I feel that the whole reality of modern living is a fraud, a distraction from some deep and living thing. Maybe we help release that in our work." He laughed, half angrily.

She gave him a mug full of black coffee, looking at him curiously.

"You were saying you have an answer to your work problems. Can you tell me? I have a fascination for science, so I am genuinely interested, you know."

"Are you? Do you care about me at all? Could you ever love me?"

"Could you ever love me, Andrew? Or is it just my dreams that you care about? I sometimes think my husband never cared about the real me. My dream side is surely impersonal —it contains all kinds of fascinating—snippets, I guess, from God knows where. The collective unconscious, I guess. But the real Rose-Jean Dempson only surfaces in waking hours."

He looked at his watch. "Listen, I'll tell you what I've told nobody. I think the unit is on to something really big. There are things which have never been done before, and we could be on to one of them.

"Scientific thought is finally acknowledging the complexity of a human being. As usual, the biological side has had to come first, with its gradual revelation of the intricately different times and cycles kept by the physical body. Since then, there's been progress in other directions, all reinforcing the same pattern.

"The further we probe into sleep and dreams, the more actual becomes the vast, rich complexity of the mind. It sometimes feels like—I sometimes feel like an explorer, trembling on the brink of an unknown world."

"That must be a wonderful experience, Andrew. I'm truly glad for you."

"We've had a whole year of frustrations. The work's got nowhere. Our findings have been challenged, as you know. Now we recognize that our earlier interpretation of the evidence was incorrect. We were working with a too-simple model of the mind. At last I can understand that we are on the threshold of something of much more startling import than I ever expected. Your dreams have helped me toward an understanding of that something."

"Oh, how totally thrilling! And what is that?"

He set his mug down and said, slowly, "Rose-Jean, I can't expect anyone but myself to grasp the entire picture yet, but I have discovered that there are several different time-flows running concurrently in the brain."

"I don't understand. Time-flows?"

"We all occasionally acknowledge different time-flows, despite the horrible supremacy of clock-time in the modern world—the clock-time I believe you were escaping from in your last dream. That's why I think you are like me. There's the light, slow time-flow of childhood, the heavy, sluggish time-flow of the mentally deranged, the time that lovers appear to abolish, the speeded-up time of drunks, the suspended time-flow of catastrophe, and others. They're not imaginary, they're genuinely different internal circuitry. I believe I shall soon have proof of that, proof that many different time-flows exist within any one mind, in the same way that various time-mechanisms coexist in the body."

Angsteed went to the window, absorbed in his vision. The campus, glimpsed here from an angle, was brightly lit. Several people were about. Some strolled leisurely, some walked briskly, one or two were running. Some went in groups and pairs. Many were solitary. Some chose the light areas, some the shadows.

She was looking at him wide-eyed. There was something curious in her manner.

"Do you mind if I draw the drapes?"

She crossed to the window. It was sunrise outside and a terrific noise was going on. The field was full of people. He understood that they were watching a comet which blazed in the sky. Attempts were being made to capture the comet in some way, in order to harness its energies for fuel.

He said, "They are going to harvest its energies."

She said, "It is not time for the harvest yet." He noticed that her husband was beside her, a small man standing behind some kind of flower arrangement.

Someone was asking what time the harvest was.

She came out from behind a rocking chair, smiling and saying that she had a record she wanted to play them over and over again.

It was already playing. It brought them all happiness. He danced with someone in the room, but it was not her. The room vanished.

They were outside, under the stars and a comet like a great biblical sheaf of wheat.

The yellow buzzer sounded.

Angsteed roused, staring around the familiar laboratory without raising his head from the pillow. He regularly used himself as his own guinea pig, and had determined to do so again directly after his evening with Rose-Jean.

He reached out almost automatically for the microphone and began to record the details of his dream, after noting the time. Early, 1:56.

He completed the report, added the words "Typical sigma dream, preoccupied with digesting the experiences of the day," and settled his head back on the pillow. Then he sat upright.

The interpretation of the dream flashed upon him. It had signaled itself as a special dream by the hint to begin with: the drawing of the curtains symbolized the closing of his eyes. And the rest . . . well, he needed to talk to someone about it. Rose-Jean! Why not? He had a pretext for visiting her at night.

Going to the dressing room, he pulled on some clothes and slippers and shuffled out of the labs. He crossed to her block. Nobody was about, although a light shone here and there where a student hunched over a book or talked to or seduced another student. The moon shone. It was a perfect night. He could hear the continuous rumble of traffic from the freeway.

Before Rose-Jean's door, he hesitated, then tried the handle. The door opened—somewhat to his surprise, for warnings about theft were posted on every residential floor. He entered. This was the room in which he had kissed her only a few hours earlier. The experience came so freshly back to him that time seemed to be annihilated.

Angsteed stood there, taking in the scents and impressions of the room before moving toward the bedroom door. Opening it, he called softly, "Rose-Jean, are you awake? It's only me, Andrew?"

He knew immediately from her tone that she had been awake. In her voice was a note almost of panic.

"Andrew? You can't come in here. It's the middle of the night. What the hell do you want?"

"I've had a dream. A revelation. I want to discuss it with you. I promise I'll only talk. Can I put the light on?"

"No! No, I forbid you to put the light on. Please go, Andrew—we can talk in the morning. I was asleep."

"But listen, darling—suddenly I've seen my way ahead, and you gave me the clue in a dream. There was a comet in the sky, and you said—"

"Andrew, will you please get out of my room before I call the porter?"

He went nearer to the bed and sat down on it, reaching for her hand. "Please attempt to listen to me. I didn't come here to seduce you! This is something really important. You know how on medical reports it is now considered vital to record at what precise time drugs are administered? The time is recognized as being as important as the amount. Because the same dosage can have widely different effects at different times of day. You told me in my dream that you had a record which was played over and over. That refers to the record of all dreams kept by the unit. We have always entered the time of waking in the sleep records, but we have not applied the time in the classificatory data. Don't you see that we can check back over the last fifteen years' records and we should be able to turn up the new factor?"

She was still angry. "You're babbling, Andrew! What new factor?"

"Didn't I say that? Look, we've studied times of dreams only as part of how long after the commencement of sleep they occur. But we need to study them as against body-time. The dreams come at certain regular intervals after the onset of sleep, but what we may have missed is that the *content* of the dreams may well be influenced by the subject's body-time! We can check on that. And my dream suggests that the answer will be epoch-making—hence, the comet. We may well discover that the different sorts of dreams come from different time-flows. In other words, it may be possible in the future to key in to whatever level of personality we require—and of course with that new understanding, we shall be able to chart an entirely new picture of consciousness!"

He leaned forward in his excitement to embrace her. The curtains were drawn together in the room. He could only vaguely discern the pale outline of her face. As he reached toward it, another face materialized next to it, and a rough male hand thrust itself into his face.

"You leave my wife alone!" a voice told him.

Next morning, Rose-Jean went to see Angsteed. She apologized for last night.

"We'd better forget it," he said. "And obviously you will want your name removed from the dream roster."

"Don't be so stuffy, Andrew. I know you sleep around a fair bit, or used to. My friends told me. Don't start being unkind to me just because I have my husband in my bed once in a while. If you must know, I didn't even invite him in last night. I thought he was hundreds of miles away, but he dropped in on me."

"I don't want to know about your personal affairs."

"Of course you do. Why sulk? Listen, Andrew, I like you a lot. I have this thing about my husband, but sooner or later I reckon I have to shake him out of my system. You can help me, if you really wish. I'm just in no mood for—oh, forget it!"

He stood against her and took her hand. "I'm sorry, Rose-Jean. Of course I'm peeved about last night, peeved with you and with *him*—and jealous, of course—and most peeved with myself. I'll get over it. Let's be friends. I need you. Think

what my life has been, stuck in dreary research institutes—
before I was here, I was studying dying flies and making moth
pupae abort in order to learn about circadian mechanisms. A
life for science! Well, it's been a living death. Your dreams
have revived me, given me new imaginative insight. I really
think I'm on the brink of a major breakthrough, and I'd like
you to get some of the excitement too."

She kissed him then.

"How's that for excitement?"

"Great. There are things which have never been done before, but they have no power to alter the essence of things."

"I don't quite see what you mean."

He looked at her in puzzlement. "Have I said that before?
Your dreams have altered something in my essence, brought
me to life in some inner way."

"I find that hard to believe; I'm so unimportant. Yet, why
not? I feel refreshed by my dreams myself, as maybe I told
you. Maybe the essence of one human life is cyclic in nature,
and a new season is about to dawn in both our psyches, if that
isn't too fanciful!"

"And a new comet in both our skies!"

At last he had broken the spell. He took her powerfully into
his arms. Their mouths met. After a moment they settled
down on Angsteed's plum-colored sofa.

The yellow buzzer woke Rose-Jean Dempson at 2:11 A.M.,
activated by her REMs.

Pulling the microphone toward her, she said, "Two-eleven.
There was an earthquake, and the university was in ruins. Everyone else seemed to have gone. It was night, and I wasn't at
all frightened.

"I ran out across the field. The layout of everything was
different. I saw a broken clock lying on the ground. It had
stopped at . . . I believe it was ten minutes past six. Evidently
it had fallen off a ruined tower.

"I went toward the line of poplars. The sky was curiously
bright and there seemed to be creatures running about near

me. One of the poplars had fallen over. I appeared to climb along its horizontal trunk. Then I was looking down at its roots, which were earthy and dangling in the air. I could see something gleaming in the hole. It was a gold casket, but when I lifted it out it had blood on it, so I gave it to someone who was beside me.

"Then it seemed that I was riding a horse. I was very excited. Maybe there was another earth tremor. It sounds silly, but the whole landscape was coming along with us. The horse started galloping around in circles.

"Reindeer were running nearby, beautiful creatures, brown and white, with terrific antlers. They ran with their heads down, breath pouring like steam from their nostrils.

"I was full of delight because in the morning the world was going to begin anew. I guess it all sounds like a typical ypsilon dream, I'm afraid."

Rose-Jean looked about the laboratory, thick with the dusk of shaded lights and the caterpillar sounds of machines. Her eyelids closed, shutting it all away. Her head went back on the pillow and she slept. Ninety-five minutes later, the yellow buzzer roused her again.

In the morning, Rose-Jean went to see her closest friend on the faculty, Alice Butley. Alice was head of the philosophy department, a stringy woman in her mid-fifties with a lot of life and humor in her. Rose-Jean had liked her from their first meeting, although Alice was almost twice Rose-Jean's age.

"Care for a drink, Rose-Jean?"

"Just a Coke, maybe."

"It's three quarters of an hour before the time for my first martini, but I guess I could run forty-five minutes ahead of schedule for once. Though 'for once' is certainly not the phrase I should use there. Drinking early is getting to be a repetitive event. . . . I can stand just so much of this place. . . . You aren't coming to tell me you're quitting?"

Rose-Jean laughed. "Far from it. I'm just getting interested.

But I guess I was wanting to talk to you about a repetitive event."

"Go ahead! This dump is stocked with nothing else but . . ."

"Alice, you'll laugh when I tell you."

"Try me."

"I think I'm falling in love with Andrew Angsteed, the head of the Dream Research Unit. Now—I know your opinion of him is mixed, and he surely does seem a bit dull at first, but when you get to know him better, why, he's just great. He's so understanding, and the work he's doing is just fascinating."

Alice brought over the drink. "It's not the work in your man's life, it's the man in your life's work that counts. Andrew's nearer my age than yours. Still, when could one ever say that and expect a hearing?"

"He really is tremendous, Alice. He's had a dull life, but now he feels that everything is going to change. I feel just the same way. Really new things are about to happen!"

Raising her glass, sipping, Alice said, "Well, there are things which have never been done before, events that have never taken place, but they have no power to alter the essence of things. You may or may not resent that, according to temperament."

"I don't follow you. You're saying the essence of things is repetitive?"

"No, but the essence of human life experience is largely a matter of repetition—or cyclic in nature, let's say, since generations do not differ in that respect, suffering the same miseries and pleasures, the same emotions, the same realities of birth, death, love, and so on. . . . Not forgetting boredom —it's a worser killer than death, as my old pop used to say."

Her phone warbled. She walked over to the desk and cut it off.

Perching on the edge of a chair, Rose-Jean said, "But these cycles—they aren't concentric, are they? I mean, otherwise the same events would happen over and over again, without the participants being aware of it."

"Well, don't they, damnit!"

Rose-Jean's gaze dropped to the floor. Then she laughed. "Maybe, I guess. At least—oh, I don't know. You're the philosopher, Alice. You see, I did want to talk to you about a repetitive event. You know the last place I was in, the University of Catrota, well, I also fell in love with a man there. He was very intelligent but sort of a hippie. No, not a hippie, but at least a potential dropout from society. He didn't accept the way society was run, any more than Andy does, in a different way. His name was Allan Dempson. We got married. I told you about it."

"Sure. You told me it didn't work out."

"Oh, we tried, but it was just impossible. He was gorgeous, but so tyrannical. Andrew's quite different. I had to leave Allan and Catrota. He's given up his job there too. He's working as a long-distance truck driver, when he works at all."

"Now you're afraid you're going to make a mess of things all over again with Andrew Angsteed?"

"I don't know. You said it yourself, the major events of life occur over and over again. Still, Allan and Andrew are so different. I guess Allan just had one major obsession, the state of society."

Alice looked at the younger woman meditatively. "I'd say that hit off Andy pretty accurately, too. He's obsessive, if ever I saw it."

"Oh—I don't know . . . I just find him so fascinating. . . ."

Alice took her arm. "Honey, you spend too long on that dream machine. You're still married to Allan, right? So you *can't* marry Andrew. That takes care of that."

"But I can divorce Allan. He said I could."

"In order to marry Andrew? Maybe your trouble is that you are pursuing archetypes, not real people. That's when the going really gets difficult and events really start to repeat themselves. Let me lend you Anna Kavan's *Ice* to read; then you'll understand what I mean by pursuit of archetypes. You are seeing Andrew generically when you should view him as an individual. Let's talk again about this—I must go and see old Birkett. We've got a deal of trouble regarding the appropriations fund."

"You've nothing against Andrew?"

Alice looked away. "No. I'm very fond of Andrew."

Angsteed shut himself in his office and played back to himself the casette on which he had recorded Rose-Jean's dream from the master tape. The master tape was university property; the casette was his property. He now had records of 174 dreams dreamed by Rose-Jean Dempson. In the work files of his department, all dreams contributed to the bank by all volunteers were anonymous, and elaborately cross-filed in the computer according to dream-type, content, key-symbol, and so on. Now they were all being additionally classified according to time of dream.

All that was impersonal, and routine. Angsteed's private collection of Rose-Jean's dreams was both private and personal.

He let his mind wander as her sleepy voice reached him through the earphone in his ear. Her dream territory had become more and more familiar to him. He, possibly more than any other man alive, was able to chart that territory. In every dream he could tell his whereabouts in her psyche, in which quadrant, how deep he was. He knew the colorations, he had come to recognize various meta-continents, in each of which certain archetypal emotion events prevailed. All was cloudy, ever-changing, but he no longer went in fear of losing his orientation. As his knowledge and sensibility increased, he grew to comprehend something about the different time-flows of the different meta-continents.

Gradually, and without being aware of it, he was coming nearer to the Heartland, that interior which no conscious thought—not even Rose-Jean's—had ever penetrated. The interior was beset with mystery and guarded with barricades, the greatest of which was the attenuation of consciousness into sleep. The effect came like an enchantment as one approached, and the brainwaves which it radiated served as tsetse fly in maintaining the territory intact and virginal. But Angsteed was learning to move in ever deeper.

During the lunch hour, he retired to his room, taking the casette to add to his growing collection. He moved slowly and somnambulistically, often ignoring the greetings of his fellows.

He had plans for writing a ballet, for making a film, for painting a picture, which would embody the inner world of which he was the sole explorer. As yet only a few notes and diagrams existed. Sometimes Angsteed sat before his typewriter, sometimes he sat with his gouaches on the desk before him. Rarely did he do more than gaze into perspectives of which only he was aware.

When his phone warbled he picked it up and spoke inattentively.

It was Rose-Jean.

At once he became more alert.

"We both have the night free of the lab. Let me drive you into Goadstown and we'll have a meal together. You might even remind me how to dance. How's about it?"

"Why, that would be fine, Andrew, but—"

"No buts, honey! Let me for once pose as a man of action. Be round at my apartment at six, and we'll have a drink before we go. I had a letter this morning that I'd like you to cast an eye over. Things are going to change from now on, and you're a part of it."

"Oh, okay, Andrew, whatever you say. Thanks."

Although he set the phone down briskly, the smile on his face faded into abstraction, and he sat where he was, gazing into his own personal distance.

He was lying on his bed with the same expression on his face when Rose-Jean arrived that evening, brightly dressed for the trip to town.

"I'd meant to be showering, but I got lost in a fit of abstraction. I'm not always quite so absentminded." He kissed her rather formally.

"You'd better go and shower now, then. I came at six, as

you asked." She was piqued that he offered no compliments about her appearance after the long ritual she had subjected herself to before her mirror.

"Sure, sure. Won't be long! Grab yourself a Coke out of the icebox. Have a look at my books."

She did as she was bid, mooching back and forth before his well-worn collection of hardcovers and paperbacks with a glass in her hand. She saw no titles that particularly took her fancy, except for some egghead movie paperbacks. The directors discussed were Bunuel, Jancso, Tarkovsky, and Bergman. Since the latter was the only one she had heard of, and his films bored her, she shoveled the volumes back into their shelf. She put a Bonzo Dog Band record on the record-player instead.

Just as Angsteed reappeared, looking unfamiliar in a gray suit, the doorbell rang. Alice Butley entered.

"Hi, Rose-Jean, you're looking great. I've picked a bad time to call, Andy—I can see you're going out. I only dropped in for an idle chat. I'll call around some other time."

"Don't go. Great to see you again, Alice. I'm just getting myself a martini—let me make you one."

"I can resist anything but temptation. Set 'em up."

When they were drinking, Angsteed said, "Alice, things are most definitely going to be different, radically different, around here. We're on the move at last. The psyche is going to expand in a big way. Believe me, I'm on to something really new, aren't I, Rose-Jean?"

"Oh, I do hope so."

"Well, there *are* things that have never been done before, though most of them are powerless to alter the essence of existence," Alice said.

"What about a new thing that goes directly to the essence of existence?" He grinned and looked at Rose-Jean for her approval.

"The essence of the human life experience is largely a matter of repetition. It's cyclic in nature, at the least, with every generation suffering the same miseries and pleasures."

"Oh, sure, we all enjoy the same emotions, the same realities of birth and death, love, desire, hate. Haven't I said that to you before?"

Rose-Jean perched on the edge of Angsteed's sofa and said, "These cycles, Alice—at least they can't be concentric, or else the same events would happen over and over again without the participants being aware of it." She passed her hand across her brow, as if brushing away a hair.

Alice laughed. "So they do happen over and over again! I guess reason suggests otherwise, but reason is fallible in these matters."

"A fine thing for a philosopher to say! You've no proof of this repetition."

She spread her hands and offered him a face of innocence. "The major events of life occur over and over, perpetually. Rose-Jean agrees with me, don't you, Rose-Jean?"

But Rose-Jean had walked over to the window and was pressing her forehead against the glass. Angsteed went quickly across to her and put an arm around her shoulders.

"What's the trouble, honey? You okay?"

"I'm okay. I just hate what we're talking about. Sometimes I get an awful sense of déjà vu. Let's go out; if we're going out —can we, do you mind?"

"Just say the word, sweetheart."

"I can take a hint," Alice said. She shot Angsteed a significant and warning look, but he chose not to heed it.

Toward midnight, they finished up at Luigi's, where the juke-box was loud, the lamps were encased in lead, and the waitresses wore green leather pants and little else. Beyond the pool tables was a space for dancing. Angsteed was drunk enough to try a few steps. He enjoyed the music and the noise and the people.

"Too long since I did this!" he shouted to her.

"It does rather look that way, Andy. Wouldn't you rather sit down?"

"Come on, girl, I'm only just getting going! You know your trouble?"

"What is my trouble?"

He started to laugh as he swayed. "You're just a babe-in-arms. You should learn to drink, that's what you should do! Coke's a kid's drink."

"I happen to like it."

"Okay, you like it. I tell you what—let me get you a Coke with rum in it. How about that?"

"No, thanks, alcohol is a drug and I'm not having any."

He stopped dancing. "What's wrong with you, Rose-Jean? What was that you said the other day about not being a person? Alcohol never did anyone any harm in moderation. Now come on, come and have a Coke and rum. What do they call it? A Cuba Libre! I'll have a Cuba Libre with you!"

He dragged her away to a table, shouting for a waitress. Finally, two Cuba Libres were brought and set before them.

"I'm not going to drink it, Andy, so you'd better make up your mind."

"What you afraid of? Come on, pour it down, honey! More where that came from!" He started his own drink, and continued until his glass was empty. Some of the liquid ran down his chin and onto his shirt. He wiped his chops with a grand gesture.

She clutched his arm. "Andy, let's get out of here. I see my husband over by the bar, and he can be real mean."

"Leave it to me. I'll take care of that bastard! Where is he? Which one's him?" He stared pugnaciously at the throng of people by the bar.

"I'm not having any fighting. I thought he was a thousand miles away. Let's get out of here fast and back home, if you're sober enough to drive."

"Balls, go and tell him to join us. Let's buy him a drink."

She put her face closer to him and said, "Andy, if you don't come out to the car this instant, I swear to you that everything is over between us from this moment on, and I will never

speak to you again. I know my husband better than you do,
and I'm telling you to come on out."

"All right, all right, I heard, relax! He won't kill us!"

"You'd be surprised!" She put her arms around Angsteed
and dragged him through the crowd and out of the saloon,
keeping her face away from the bar. Angsteed tried to deter-
mine whom they were avoiding, but, as far as he could see,
none of the people at the bar were taking any notice of them.

Outside, they made their way through the parking lot to
Angsteed's car. Angsteed was argumentative and wanted to
return to give Dempson a going-over; Rose-Jean had some
difficulty in getting him into the driving seat.

"Please drive carefully, Andy! Oh, you look so wild!"

He steered a way slowly through the lot and toward the
main entrance. As they came under the fake carriage lights at
the gate, Rose-Jean cried that she could see Dempson, head
down, walking toward the exit.

With a roar, Angsteed threw the vehicle forward. Rose-
Jean screamed. A man in their path turned and jumped to one
side, and the off-wing of the vehicle rammed a brick pillar.
Sounds of falling glass as one of the headlights went out. Au-
tomobiles behind began hooting. Both Angsteed and Rose-
Jean jumped out to inspect the damage.

"You were going to run him over, you madman!"

"No, I wasn't. I only meant to give him a scare."

"When I got a proper look at him I saw it wasn't Allan anyway."

In her arms later, the drink still in him, he cried in self-
hatred, "What sort of a man am I? Is there a curse on me,
something I can't get free from? How wretched, how circum-
scribed, my goddamned life is!"

"Don't talk so loud, Andy! You'll give me a bad reputation."

"I love you, Rose-Jean, you're marvelous, you're natural in
a way I could never be. I want to please you, yet all I do
works against our relationship. A repetitive event, like Alice

says. Anything I love, it dies on me. Even now, even saying what I am saying, I'm conscious that I may be driving us further apart."

"I love having you in my bed, Andy. It gets lonely. Did you ever make love to Alice?"

"What the hell kind of question is that? What's that got to do with what we're talking about?"

"What are we talking about? I don't know. I'm not really intellectual, as you seem to think. I mean, people are what they are, aren't they?" She started to stroke him. Finally, her hands and her kisses had their proper effect, and they filled her narrow bed with loving.

She fell asleep before he did. Angsteed lay huddled against her, claustrophobic in her narrow room, yet relishing the experience of having his head on the same pillow as that other head, which contained—or projected—a world he regarded as much more splendid than reality.

Gradually, eyes still open, he built up, in his dream cartography, a misty globe not unlike a celestial globe, with quadrants, sectors, and mythological figures scrawled over it, every one with its own intense magic. This was Rose-Jean's personal globe. What puzzled him was how it related to her personally, how far it was beyond her or even antithetical to her, how far it was on completely another plane from her own limited consciousness. That puzzlement faded as he lowered himself into the unlimited globe; his own reactions were dimmed out under the kaleidoscope of emotions in which he found himself moving.

At first, it was as if he were running amid a herd of reindeer in a storm—either a snow blizzard or a sand storm. Glittering particles obscured almost everything. Shaggy things stood to one side, fir trees of which neither boles nor crowns were visible. The eyes of the reindeer were yellow in their melancholy faces.

The colors blended perfectly. He was moving nearer the source. Currents of heat served as compass-bearings. Somewhere ahead were the mountainous heartlands, living under different times, different suns. People and animals were transformed there.

Already the process was happening about him. As he bent his head to climb, the reindeer were going into people, the people going into animals, coming out, going in again, eating and being eaten, diving into what appeared to be the ground, springing up again like divers, their movements beautiful and horrific. He tried to look into the faces of the people, which somehow eluded him. He could tell that some were unaffected by the majestic process and walked with sunshades or in flowing robes.

Someone was running beside him, matching him stride for stride. Under the jogging hair, eyes, lambent. A hint about the mouth of—what? Joy, lust, laughter, despair? Together, they came to a narrowing way, where windows loomed above them like the luminiferous eyes of fish.

He felt his heart hammering as darkness, heat, walls confined him. Now he was in a house, and someone was explaining—or attempting to explain—that this house was all there was, anywhere, that it was coextensive with the universe. The being beside him was denying the explanation.

"It's the other way about—the universe is in the house."

They sat down, on furniture scarcely indicated, and a woman entered the room. She was tall, she came toward them bearing a precious gift, something that changed shape so that they hardly comprehended. The woman's motion also set into being other shape changes. The room itself, responding to her, began to grow tremendously tall and the walls to become soft, so that he clenched his hands and felt the pulse in them like a spring.

She came and looked him in the face. The other had gone. The room was more like the hollow trunk of a tree—and more and more, until her eyes and face seemed like leaves and he became part of her and they were both merely patterns on the sinuous green growth.

"Just a minute," Alice mumbled. "Who is it? What time is it?"

She threw on a gown and padded over to her outer door. Rose-Jean was standing there. Night lay behind her in the corridor.

"Rose-Jean? What's the matter? I feel such a mess. What time is it?"

The girl was near to tears.

"Oh, Alice, I'm in such trouble! It's Andrew, please help me. He's unconscious or something and I can't wake him up. Maybe he's dying. I've tried pouring water on his face and everything."

"Jesus Christ, child, try whiskey, try the college quack, or the shrink, or the fire department—just don't try me. Andy's not my responsibility!"

"But he may be dying. People do die!"

"You don't have to wake me in the small hours to tell me that. I know people die. That's never been news!"

She backed into her room and started to search for cigarettes. Rose-Jean followed her around. Darkness lay outside the windows.

"The trouble is, Alice—I had to come to you. I'm in trouble. Andrew's blacked out in my bed." She laughed feebly, in apology.

Alice looked at her. Still looking at her, she lit a cigarette, sucked in the smoke, began to laugh and cough. Finally she managed to speak.

"Gee, that's sweet, that's just sweet! Oh, Rosie, you kill me! Poor Andy was never too much of a lover, and I guess you just wore him out. He's catching up on his beauty sleep, that's all. Now you trot on back to him and leave me to my beauty sleep—if that's the phrase I'm looking for any longer."

"Alice, please—there's something really wrong with Andy. I know it."

"There's something wrong with him, all right," Alice said, as she stared down at Angsteed a few minutes later. She lifted one of his eyelids and watched it fall back into place. "Did you hit him?"

"Of course not. At least he's not dead. Is he dying, do you

imagine? How are we going to get him to his room without anyone seeing us?"

"Can't be done. I'll phone Dr. Norris for you. He's a nice discreet guy."

Angsteed lay curled in Rose-Jean's bed, his face colorless, his lips slightly parted, hardly seeming to breathe.

"Catatonia if I ever saw it," Dr. Norris said when he arrived. He rolled Angsteed over onto his back. Angsteed lay awkwardly in the new position, unmoving.

"What happened to him?" Rose-Jean asked.

"Can't say yet. We'll have to get him to the hospital."

"Seems a pity," Alice said. "Must be something two women could do here with an absolutely helpless man. I'm sure we'd think of something."

THREE INTERVIEWS

Interview A.   Mrs. Rose-Jean Dempson.

INTERVIEWER: Mrs. Dempson, Andrew Angsteed has now been in a condition of schizophrenic withdrawal for forty-one days. On occasions he shows some awareness of his surroundings, but he will not communicate. We hope by talking to some people who know him well that we may be able to help him. Did you at any time hear him say anything which led you to suspect that he was suffering from mental stress?

ROSE-JEAN: Why, no, he was perfectly fine, I mean he was so intellectual that I doubt if I—well, he could be violent, I suppose. But what's violent? It's a violent world, isn't it?

INTERVIEWER: In what way was he violent? Did he hit you?

ROSE-JEAN: Hit me? What makes you say that? I don't give anyone cause to hit me. Besides, Andy was pretty gentle, I guess. Too gentle, really; he was sort of withdrawn, now that I come to think of it—not in any nasty way, of course. But I wouldn't call him violent. He ran his automobile into a gatepost, that I do know. Broke the headlights on the driver's side.

INTERVIEWER: Was that an accident?

ROSE-JEAN: No, that was deliberate! (*Laughs*) You see, he was drunk that night. We were driving out of a nightclub and he thought he saw my husband—did I tell you I was married? My husband and I live apart. I told Andy it wasn't Allan. I said, "Allan's in Detroit, you loon!" but he was drunk, and he drove the car at the man. The man jumped clear and Andy ran into the gatepost. Just an accident, of course.

INTERVIEWER: Was Angsteed often drunk?

ROSE-JEAN: Not to my knowledge. He was too wrapped up in the dream project. I don't drink at all myself. He was on the verge of a breakthrough when—when *this* happened. He was on a verge of a breakthrough that was about to change the world, so he said.

INTERVIEWER: Do you know what he imagined this breakthrough to be?

ROSE-JEAN: It was going to be something entirely new. I think he said he wanted to alter the essence of things. Could a new thing alter the essence of things? I seem to remember somone telling me that human life was cyclic. (*Pause*) Anyhow, about this breakdown, this *breakthrough,* I mean, of Andy's, he had some new idea about timing people's dreams in relation to their circadian mechanisms. That was somehow going to show that we have all sorts of different times going on in our heads at once. I forget the details, but that was it in general.

INTERVIEWER: Did you regard this as a feasible idea?

ROSE-JEAN: I used to contribute my dreams. I was one of his guinea pigs. That was how we met, really.

INTERVIEWER: Did you believe in Andrew's theories or did you think they might be illusions?

ROSE-JEAN: Oh, he didn't know that himself. He was just working along a scientific hypothesis. I guess a lot of things sound nutty before they're proved, don't they? Like people didn't used to believe in acupuncture, except for the Chinese, I mean, until modern science showed how it all worked. But Andy's ideas weren't way-out to me. I went to Europe for vacation once, and got most terrible jet lag, so I know there are different times in the body. Maybe Andy found a time he liked best and settled for that. Maybe we shouldn't disturb him.

INTERVIEWER: You think he is happy as he is?

ROSE-JEAN: Golly, who's ever happy? I just meant—well, I don't know what I meant. I mean, maybe Andy isn't sick—maybe he made his breakthrough. You people at the mental hospital ought to see how his brain waves register. But just don't fool around with him. I'd say—I know you don't want my advice—but I'd say let him be as he is. He could be happy, who knows, properly looked after. Gosh, *I'm* happy, don't think I'm not, but—well, it's nice to be looked after, isn't it?

Interview B.   Miss Alice Butley.

INTERVIEWER: It's good of you to see me in your lunch hour, Miss Butley.

ALICE: Who wants to hang around this place? What can I tell you about Andrew Angsteed? He's real sick, is he?

INTERVIEWER: We are curious to know why he went into a state of complete withdrawal just when he was excited by new things he was discovering.

ALICE: "New" is a relative term. As a philosopher, I distrust it. Everyone's hot for the new, the novel. I'll tell you what my old man used to say—I've got a great admiration for my old man, and I don't care who hears me say it—he used to say, "Boffers (that was his nickname for me, kind of a baby-name), Boffers, if it's new, it won't last, and if it's lasted, then it's not new." Andy wanted to find something new, something to weary people's minds with. I told him, nothing new is going to alter the essence of things.

INTERVIEWER: I believe that Angsteed claimed his discoveries could affect the essence of things.

ALICE: Don't make the mistake he made. Say what you will, the essence of the human experience is cyclic. It's largely a matter of repetition, with every generation suffering the same basic joys and sorrows.

INTERVIEWER: You're not suggesting that Angsteed has suffered from this sort of withdrawal before?

ALICE: How do I know? I haven't known him all that long or all that well.

INTERVIEWER: But you were lovers at one time?

ALICE: Be your age! Does that have to mean I know him well? He was always a closed guy. He never knew me, never took any interest in me as a person. Yet I was prepared to love him —my mother died when I was just a girl, so I was always chock full of love to give to the right person, don't believe otherwise. And we did have a bond in common. . . . Oh well . . .

INTERVIEWER: You were going to say?

ALICE: Things sound silly in daylight to strangers that seem important whispered in bed at night. The idea of philosophy is to knock the silliness out of things. But why not say it? Andy had an older sister die when he was eight years old. She drowned in a lake at a summer camp. He always said it marked him for good. He really loved that sister. Still—not quite so much drama in that as losing your dear old Ma, even if she did tan your hide, is there? (*Pause*) I guess we'd all like to withdraw at times—on full pay, of course. Was Andy's trouble sexual or to do with his work? Or both?

INTERVIEWER: We hoped you'd tell us.

ALICE: Well, I don't know. Is that thing switched off? Maybe I shouldn't suggest this, but all this business with dreams, it could have become obsessive with Andy. Who knows, maybe he vanished into the recesses of his own mind. Maybe he's *happy* where he is! (*Laughs*)

INTERVIEWER: Mrs. Dempson suggested the same thing.

ALICE: She did? She's hardly the person to know about such things. A little immature for such speculations, wouldn't you say?

Interview C.   The Author.

INTERVIEWER: Mr. Aldiss, the interviews with Miss Butley and Mrs. Dempson didn't get us very far. Don't you feel both ladies could have been more revealing?

AUTHOR: No. I thought they were very revealing about themselves. I agree they produced no astonishing revelations about Angsteed, but then that's the way life goes.

INTERVIEWER: This is a story, not life. Do you intend to finish the story without telling the reader what happened to Angsteed? Did he have some sort of personality collapse, or did he actually find his way into a dream world?

AUTHOR: It's a good question. You are asking me, in effect, whether this is a sad story or a happy one. I believe you are also asking me whether it is a science fiction story or not.

INTERVIEWER: I wasn't aware of so doing. Like Miss Butley and Mrs. Dempson, you wish to talk about yourself?

AUTHOR: Not at all. Unlike those ladies, I am intensely interested in Angsteed as a person. You see, I know him. He is an actual person, although I have changed a few details to protect the parties involved, as they say. And I have a particular reason for ending the story here and now: because the real Angsteed is still in his state of schizophrenic withdrawal, or however you care to label it. So the resolution has yet to come.

INTERVIEWER: May I say on behalf of the reader that I think it might have been a better story if you had waited till the resolution came?

AUTHOR: Ah, but then the quality of my interest would change and you would get a different story. A science fiction writer is like a journalist in that respect—he gets hooked on something that is still happening. The mystery intrigues him just as much as the solution. However, I have no wish to cheat. Far from it. Let me give you not one but two possible endings, just briefly. Okay?

INTERVIEWER: Go ahead.

AUTHOR: Right. First the sad ending, the non-SF ending.

Eventually, Angsteed is brought out of his withdrawal. He seems not quite as he was before, and is reluctant to return to the university. He is kept on at the mental institution for some while, but shows little interest in the outside world. His prognosis is not favorable. As for the diagnosis, while it is couched in abstruse and precise-sounding terms, it actually reveals little.

Angsteed, it says, has suffered a mental collapse caused primarily by overwork. Rose-Jean has inadvertently brought about the crisis point. Angsteed wanted her love, while realizing that he and she were nevertheless incompatible.

His "case history," slowly compiled from various sources, reveals a number of affairs over the years with older women, Alice Butley being his most recent involvement. Rose-Jean, a younger woman, is identified in his mind with his dead sister. The terms "incest fixation" and "guilt association" are bandied about.

INTERVIEWER: And Angsteed's promising line of dream research?

AUTHOR: There was no promising line. The dream research was getting nowhere; Angsteed's fantasies of imminent revolutionary discoveries were to protect himself from knowledge of yet another failure. The unit is closed down shortly after his breakdown and its appropriations reassigned.

INTERVIEWER: There had been other failures in his life?

AUTHOR: The essence of human experience is cyclic, you know.

INTERVIEWER: Do things work out better in the alternate ending?

AUTHOR: Oh, much better. The first story, you see, is just a little downbeat study of character. Whereas the science fiction story, the story with the happy ending, is an upbeat study of ideas. Whereas Angsteed's theories prove, in the first story, to be just a paranoid fixation, in the SF story they are proved to be true.

INTERVIEWER: True?

AUTHOR: Yes, true—part of the external world. A whole range of SF stories operate like that: the screwy ideas, instead of being certifiable, turn out to mirror true reality. The hero is proved right and everyone else is proved wrong, from Aristotle onward. Paranoia triumphs, logic is defeated. That's one of the reasons why outsiders believe SF to be a load of nonsense. Why did Angsteed so enjoy Rose-Jean's dreams? Because they strengthened his growing conviction that the "cold sane," as he called them, were deluded and that the mad were really the sane.

INTERVIEWER: Yes, but that was just his interpretation of her dreams.

AUTHOR: That's what I'm trying to say. To my mind, interpretation is everything—and not merely in my story. However, here's how the second version goes.

Angsteed comes out of his withdrawal in a few weeks. He remains quiet and reserved, but is again in control of himself. Since his post remains open for him, he returns to the university.

He is as convinced as ever that he has—no, I'd better phrase this with care—he is aware that his consciousness penetrated into Dream Time. "Dream Time" is his phrase for it. Dream Time is obviously akin to Jung's "Collective Unconscious."

The place he went to was no particular place—not in Rose-Jean's mind, not his own mind, although her dreams gave him the key he needed. He regards that as important: that he was in some impersonal place.

He feels sure that many other people have been there, often maybe in one form or another of madness, where time-displacement is a familiar phenomenon; but those people were unable to recognize where they had been.

"My conception of a dream globe enabled me to navigate, and to control my consciousness deeper into the Heartland than anyone else had ever been," he says. "I return just as out of madness, as a person reborn. I feel older, wiser, replenished at source, as people do after sleep and dreams."

"You're a real pioneer, Andy," says Rose-Jean. "An astronaut, no less!"

"In a sense I've discovered nothing new," he says. "Yet I know that when I come to publish my findings, a slow revolution in human thought will be set in motion, a unifying revolution that will make us revise our ideas about the unity of human life, not only in waking and sleep, in madness and sanity, but one with another. Eventually, everyone will be able to visit the Heartland and replenish themselves."

"The problem with the human race is that it needs to wake up, not go further asleep," says Alice. " 'Sing heigh-ho, the wind and the roses, This life damn soon closes!' . . ."

"It won't be like that, Alice. We will no longer be cut off from our inner beings. It's nearer immortality than death, believe me! Maybe madness and psychosis and neurosis and the rest will fade away in a couple of generations. Why the human race was barred from its own Heartland for a million years, we don't know. Maybe we'll find out now. Maybe it was necessary for growing purposes—like an adolescent's quarrel with his family. Now we're back, back to an entirely new vision of reality. At last we're going to be able to change the essence of things."

"It sounds marvelous," says Rose-Jean. She hugs him.

"Sounds too good to be true," says Alice. She laughs.

She pours them drinks. Martinis for her and Angsteed, a Coke for Rose-Jean.

*The wonders of new technologies are given first to the rich,
and only after the jet-set has sampled them do prices come down
to a level most of us can afford. Which means that the rich serve
as technology-tasters for us in much the same way servants were
once used to make sure their monarchs' food wasn't poisoned.
Considering that too rich a diet of new wonders can cause the
disease of ennui, maybe we should be thankful for this situation.
See, for instance, the following pungent serving of technology
on wry.*

GORDON EKLUND *and* GREGORY BENFORD *have published two
previous collaborations in* Universe; *the most recent was their
Nebula Award-winning novelette in* ⅍4, If The Stars Are Gods.

What Did You Do Last Year?

BY GORDON EKLUND & GREGORY BENFORD

They waited impatiently, David Golden and his young bride,
Melody, beneath the colossal dome. Their table was private,
away from the rabble. Overhead were stars, drifting slowly
through a swirl of color. David drummed his fingers, wishing
his sister Carol would arrive with her lout of a husband.

Melody's head craned back, watching the display in the
dome and oblivious to the low murmur of voices. David
nudged his chair and it said, "—in the central region. Blue
from hydrogen, red from oxy radicals. This is an emission
nebula, its fluorescence fed by ultraviolent from the young,
hot stars embedded in the dust. Explorers—"

He wasn't sure this new place, the Castle Orion, was going
to work out at all. God, what confusing stuff. He ignored Melody, still looking, and searched the crowd for Carol, his twin.
January 31, she couldn't have forgotten. And if she had—was
it calculated? No, no one forgets his birthday.

"You must be really eager," Melody said. Her excited gaze flickered past the undisciplined mass of human flesh that circulated through the public portion of the ballroom. "David, tell me, how long has it been? Not a whole year? You two must have so much to say."

"No, nothing." He glanced up to where, upon the black interior of the dome, a glittering message was burning into existence. "Not that I can think of."

"Well, I certainly am," Melody said, gazing up too. But it was only a commercial. Tomorrow, come noon, an electrical man would implode himself. Seats were available on a strictly reserved basis, with priority going to the better listings. David burped. He had witnessed so many electrical men imploding themselves that he was afraid to start counting.

He drank his liquor through a pale thin straw. "The time?" he asked, as two nearly naked men—one in hot pursuit of the other—crossed the top of their table.

"Nearly eleven," said Melody when the men had passed. "David, are you sure they haven't—"

"Oh, Lord, they're here," he said, waving into the shifting crowd that dangled in the public air. Carol came floating toward them. Except for a neat triangle of painted breasts she could have been him. Even their hair—midnight-black and trimmed exactly to the shoulders—was the same. Behind her Carol drew a large hairy man dressed in African jewelry. Otherwise naked, the man was artificially enhanced, a huge thing dangling past the kneecap.

"Is that—" Melody said, refusing to conceal her astonishment.

"For God's sake, sit down," David said. "It's Garth—yes."

"Why, they're . . . they're marvelous."

"I hadn't noticed." Deliberately he turned away, facing the floorshow. A man in uniform holding a long bloody sword was disemboweling a naked child. A historical spectacle. Good God! How many times had he seen this one before?

"Carol," he murmured, turning back.

"Happy, happy, happy," Carol said, touching David's mouth. Their lips, identical in shape and color, slid neatly together.

Distantly, Melody cried her approval. Drawing back from his sister, David mechanically said, "Shut up, Melody."

"No!" Carol cried. She pointed across the table. "David—don't tell me. Is that her?"

"So they tell me."

"Oh, but, David, why did you do it? Wasn't there any other way?"

Melody was chattering at Garth, who slowly stroked his forearm hair with a white fish-skeleton comb. His massive, animal silence made Melody speak faster. David made an effort to deflect the conversation: "I see Garth hasn't changed."

"Should he? But her. Her? Why her? David, surely you didn't—"

"I did." Calmly he removed a cigarette from his tin nose. "Advancement. Her father happens—"

"Oh, him—her." Carol wiped a tear from her eye. "Oh, Christ, David, I'm sorry—I forgot."

"So what did you do last year?" Carol asked David. All four were seated at the table. Garth fingered Melody's silvered dorsal fins in explicit invitation, using his thumbnail to advantage.

"Not much. It was—"

"We had a marvelous time on our honeymoon," Melody interrupted. "It was really fun, wasn't it?"

Carol cocked an amazed eyebrow at David, who shrugged. "Dr. Divine," he said.

"The teledream treatment."

"You've heard of him?" he asked, surprised.

"Hasn't everyone?"

Again Melody interrupted. "Dr. Divine shot us both full of wild, wild dope. And hypnosis. You wouldn't believe his eyes. They were like—like big black swimming pools. And his —yipe."

Garth had bitten her nipple off.

David, shrugging apologetically, went on: "Some old story. Pure fiction. Where does he get them? I was the Pope and Melody—"

"A wild robot." Escaping Garth, she had risen above the table, where she drifted, hands flashing excitedly. "I was really him—the robot—and he wasn't even a real person. We fought sword duels and rode donkeys and you couldn't tell it wasn't real life."

"And you, David?" Carol asked. "You were involved in this too?"

"Yes," he said defensively.

"And was it the way Melody describes?" She made no effort to keep the sarcasm from creeping into her tone. "Was it marvelous? Fantastic? Was it utterly real?"

"It was," David said, "an absolute bore."

"Of course." Carol giggled.

"And"—getting up his nerve—"and you, Carol? What did you do last year?"

"Dr. Divine."

"The same?" He allowed himself a brief, relieved smile, though not yet triumphant. "How was it? Which story did you live?"

Carol turned away, distracted. Following her gaze, David caught sight of Garth and Melody taking the tumble slide through the ice-crystal clouds above. A hollow gong; the crystals dissolved into a rain of acrid fire.

"Story? Did you say story? David, David." Reaching out, she patted his hand tenderly. "That was ages ago when they were doing stories. It's people now—real people. Dr. Divine transmits your soul into another body. Garth and I were—can you fashion it?—a San Francisco streetcleaner and his mistress. Oh." She rocked in her chair, nearly laughing. "It was tremendously amusing."

Tilting forward, shoving her hand aside, he cried: "You mean to say you liked it?"

She laughed in high, shrill, stuttering giggles. "Oh, God,

David, how could I? Streetcleaning—oh, oh, oh." She giggled on. "It was a dreadful bore."

"I see." He drew back. Above, Melody, losing her balance, toppled down toward the tabletop. The brittle plastic shattered easily. Drinks, food, candlesticks—everything flew into the orange cloud forming for the next slide. The table collapsed. Gratefully, David sank to his knees in the soft carpet and stayed there.

"It's nearly twelve," Carol announced when the new table arrived. "We'd better vault." She fluttered immediately into the air, calling back to David, "See you there."

Gulping his drink, Garth hurried after her.

"Now what?" Melody asked, wide-eyed.

David shook his head, remembering how Dr. Divine had assured him that the teledream treatment was a secret process. The filthy liar. "We vault."

"To where? Where now?"

"Chicago," he said, staggering to his feet.

She bounced up to join him. "Why there?"

"Because it's eleven o'clock there." Together they were passing through the crowd. "Then, in an hour, we go to Denver. Then San Francisco. Anchorage. Honolulu. And so on."

"That's marvelous. How long can it last?"

"As long as you want it," he said glumly. They had reached the vaulting booths. He spied Garth's hairy flanks disappearing inside one sealed cage. But a long line stretched ahead of him and Melody.

"And then what?" she said.

"Then you go home."

"Home?"

"Yes." He added, pleasantly, "With Garth."

"No!" Her terror was genuine. "Me—with him?"

"Oh, he's as tender as a lamb," David assured her. "As gentle as a child."

"But what—?"

"About me?" David said, substituting his own question for her unspoken one. "Well, I'll tell you." Her vulgarity, after all, deserved some reward. Why should he suffer alone? "I'm going to take Carol home with me. It's a tradition with us—an old family tradition."

"I've really been looking forward to tonight," Melody confessed as she and David passed through the thick, shifting mob of the memorial ballroom. "Last year was fun."

"You enjoyed it?"

"Oh, yes."

"Does that mean you enjoyed Garth?" He smiled pleasantly at her.

"Oh"—she looked deliberately away—"frap you."

He laughed. The size of the crowd here tonight depressed him. The Castle Orion had become increasingly common as its popularity grew. Some of the people he saw here tonight were incredible in their base coarseness. Compared to them, Melody might be elected to serve as a symbol of elegant sophistication. "Float up and see if they're here," he told her, but as soon as he spoke he spotted Carol and Garth seated at a table in the private section of the room. Swiftly he and Melody slid into the chairs reserved for them.

"Happy, happy, happy," Carol said, meeting his lips.

A moment later Melody darted off, murmuring something. Garth polarized himself into two fundamental colors and blended instantly with the dank, humid jungle that was forming around their table. A panther snarled. David saw the cat eyes gleaming beneath the folds of a wet elephant-ear leaf. The fern trembled and he saw that it was Garth, seeking Melody.

"Some things never seem to change," Carol said.

"You must mean Melody."

"No better?"

He shrugged. "I think she's hopeless."

"Oh, David." Carol grabbed his hand, pressing fervently. "You have to keep trying. Otherwise, what's the use? Live each moment of your life to its fullest. Never do anything twice because there isn't enough time to do it all once. I know I told you last year—I sense a real core of seriousness below all that vulgar veneer."

"I remember," he lied.

"But—tell me—what have you been doing this year?"

It had come too quickly for him. He took a deep sour breath, hoping she failed to detect the depth of his anxiety. A water sphere burst nearby and Melody dropped beside him. Her presence served only to deepen his fear.

"Dr. Divine—" Melody suddenly began.

David couldn't help himself. Her words— He struck her viciously across the face. A white spot formed on her cheek. A scarlet trickle of blood ran from her nose. "Oh, David," she said, burying her face in the white tablecloth.

"For Christ's sake, quit whimpering," he said.

"You didn't answer my question," Carol said.

He waved at Melody "She already did. Dr. Divine. But"—he tried to inject a note of confidence into his voice—"it was different."

"How so? Real people?"

"Oh, that was last year. This year we were—" He paused for effect.

"Monsters," Melody concluded, holding her bleeding nose between two fingers.

"She means aliens," he added quickly.

"Oh, really?" Carol said. "And how was that?"

"Interesting," he said, choosing his language with care. "The soul is transported across space. We spent a few months on a dust planet. A real place, too. We read the expeditionary report first."

"It was fun?" Carol asked coldly.

"Yes," Melody said. She breathed out, spattering her face with tiny droplets of blood that quickly turned brown. She ignored it, but her chin trembled. "So—so different."

"I see," Carol said.

"It was a bore," David said. "Awful." He affected a weary laugh. "Slithering through the hot sand like worms. Ugh."

"Then," said Carol, "you missed the real excitement last year."

"I did?" David said.

"Oh, yes. Haven't you heard? The starlanes are finally open, really open. Garth and I had seats on the first flight. Quaint places, I can hardly recall the names. Oh, Sirius—a big star. The light hurts your eyes. Some had aliens like yours. Interesting, yes . . . but, well, stupid."

"Some alien races are quite intelligent," Melody said.

"Are they?" Carol said. "If you want, you might be able to get reservations. See for yourself."

"Not this year," David said.

"Oh, David," Melody cried. "Couldn't we?"

"David," said Melody, sighing peevishly, "why won't you tell her? I think it's mean of you to make her wait." Melody's hands glowed brightly. She was wearing a pair of electronically enhanced gloves—a rage only slightly out of fashion—and they had so far proven useful in keeping Garth at a distance. Presently he writhed on the floor, clutching his genitals with both hands. "It was a marvelous time we had. Don't be ashamed."

"I loathe this place," David said, concentrating upon Carol to the exclusion of all else. "Next year, we go somewhere else."

"That's next year," Carol said. "I want to know what you did last year."

"Oh, please tell her," said Melody.

"We took a spaceride," he said.

"Oh," Carol said, plainly disappointed. "You mean the stars."

He nodded.

"Garth and I did that too." She waved a hand. "Ages ago, of course."

"We didn't really go to the stars," he said.

"You were lying to me?"

"No, not really. We went through the stars—not to them. We went—"

"To where there is nothing," Melody said, her voice filled with awe.

His glare silenced her. "To the edge of the universe," he explained. "Where there is nothing. The stars got redder and redder. There were galaxies going by. Everything was older and fainter. Murkey. They told us we were approaching the edge of the observable universe, out beyond where men can see—"

"Why can't you see farther?" Carol said.

"Something, I didn't catch it. Some jargon, you know. We left a week after last birthday—it takes that long. We arrived home two days ago."

"It was unbelievable," Melody said. "Utterly."

"It was nothing," David said. "Utterly." He laughed. "But isn't that the whole point? The edge of the universe—nothing. The trip was interesting, though the service was poor, the food crude, the robots sloppy. The actual arrival was a monstrous letdown. What can you do with nothing?"

"It was scary," Melody said, shivering.

David nodded, as if agreeing, then reached over and touched the control that powered her gloves. Immediately, the light went out. In response, Garth bounced off the floor. He growled and sprang at Melody. Shrieking, she danced away. Garth flew after her.

David, smiling sourly, continued: "Nothing."

But Carol was no longer listening. "We had a vaguely interesting time ourselves. But we're through with space. Now it's time instead."

"Time?"

"Travel. Haven't you heard? Dr. Proteus in Rio. Oh"—her smooth face wrinkled in anxious thought—"I just can't remember where. Or when. The past is like a lunar landscape. All craters look the same. Wars, plagues, assassinations, earthquakes, scandals, floods. Who cares? Dr. Proteus wanted to send us to old America but I said no to that. I think we went somewhere in France. It was just what I expected. Peasants gathering faggots, and who needs that?"

"Yes," David said.

"But I am beginning to worry about you. David, I want you to tell me the truth. Is it"—she lowered her voice to a confidential whisper—"her? Does she force you?"

"What?" He didn't understand.

"Is it her who makes you take all these absurd trips?"

"No," David said dully. He stood up, scanning the room. "Melody never forces me to do anything."

The four of them sat around a small, stained wooden table. Between them, untouched, sat four mugs of dark, odiferous beer. The room was barely occupied. A shabby trio clustered near a table in one shadowed corner. The air held the flat, oily memory of yesterday's fried food. The bartender held his post at a crude barswell. Behind the bar, fastened to a cloudy mirror, a sign said: WE RESERVE THE RIGHT TO REFUSE SERVICE TO ANYONE.

Reading the words aloud, Carol giggled. "Do you suppose," she asked, "they mean us?"

David blushed. "I thought it would be a change."

"Oh, it is." She turned her head slowly, as if dazzled by the atmosphere. "It is."

"I mean—"

"Six months ago it would have been all right. But, David, these places are too blatantly quaint. They never were able to catch on."

"It is nice," Melody said. "Sort of serene. Even Garth is quiet."

"That," Carol said, "is because he's falling asleep—from boredom."

"I was sick of the Castle Orion," David said. "I couldn't stand that place another year."

"Oh, they've improved it," Carol said. "Finally. It's much

more exclusive now. The ax fell last month. Why, David"—
she laughed gaily—"I'm not even sure you could get in now."

"Don't say that. Just—just shut up." He pouted, turning
sullen.

Carol patted his hand. "Oh, oh, oh," she said softly. "But"
—she smiled—"no matter. In an hour, Chicago. Before then,
though, I want to know what you did last year."

"Dr.—"

"Not Divine?"

He shook his head. "Proteus."

"Oh, him," Carol said, covering her lips. "Garth, you remember. When was it we—?"

David hurried on: "We went all the way back."

"Cave men?"

"Before that."

"Dinosaurs?"

"Before that."

"Well, when?"

"Past the edge of time. To the dawn of creation. We saw
the earth being born."

"It was—" Melody began, but, catching a glimpse of
David, she fell silent.

"Well," said Carol, "tell me. How was it?"

"Gas," David said, recollecting slowly. "Swirling mists. Everything a dull red, like embers. Interesting—in an intellectual way—but—"

She sighed. "It was the same with Garth and me. We
died."

"What?" cried Melody. "You died? Do tell us."

"Yes," David said painfully, "do."

"A new technique. Dr. Divine. You die—and it isn't pretty
—he guarantees that—what a morbid imagination—and then
you are revived. How many times did we die, Garth? Eight?
Nine?"

"And was it interesting?" David said, his tone almost ugly.
"Did you have a simply lovely time?"

Carol ignored his mood. "Being reborn was rather fun," she

said, "but dying—" She made an ugly face. "It's something I could've lived without." She laughed joyously and David swallowed a fierce gulp of beer. Suddenly, swiveling in her chair, Carol threw her arms around Melody's bare shoulders and kissed her lips. "Oh, Melody," she cried, jumping up. "You and David are my two favorite people. Hurry, hurry." She tugged Melody with her. "We don't want to be late."

"I can't see them," Melody said flatly.

"They're here," David said.

"I still don't see them." They stood side by side upon the memorial-ballroom floor of the Castle Orion. Gazing around —his view distinctly limited—David was appalled. The room was densely packed. The customers seemed lower than any he remembered from the past.

"Let's find our table," he said. "They may be there."

"All right." She shrugged. "If you insist."

He stopped and glared. "What do you mean by that? What do you think we should do? Just turn around? Go straight home?"

"I couldn't care less."

"Last year you seemed to care."

"Oh, oh, oh," she said softly. "You were the one who chose the beer garden."

"But you chose to go home."

"David, David," she cried, laughing shrilly. Suddenly, stretching forward on tiptoes, she patted his pale cheek. "Wasn't he tender as a lamb? Wasn't he gentle as a child?"

"Leave me alone. You'll never understand."

They had barely reached the edge of the public arena. Melody abruptly darted away into the crowded sky, slipping between a writhing quartet of air-lovers. David would not follow. As he walked he passed through private clouds, becoming a flitting intruder in a courtyard; a dungeon; star cluster; a swirling air fight between winged demons; an accountant's office. In the aisle he met a grinning panda bear with a tennis racket, but waved away the animal's whispered proposition. Someone offered him a drink; he slid it into his wrist. A plasma frog was rushed ahead of him. They only lived three months, so he supposed the practice was justified. A coronal discharge covered a shriek, a gurgle, some muffled struggling. When he reached the table he found Melody sitting alone.

"What a stupid frapping waste that was," he said.

"What was?" she asked innocently.

"Your flying ahead to see her first."

"Oh, David." She flung both hands into the misty air. "You know I loathe walking."

Silently, through a pale thin straw, he drank his liquor. Maybe she was right. Maybe this whole birthday celebration had degenerated into a hopeless waste. For weeks before and after, he was good for nothing else.

"Just remember what I said," he warned her.

"Oh, frap you."

"Just don't forget."

"Oh, frap."

Soon enough, they came. Garth, ageless, appeared first, dressed in his usual glittering array of raw jewelry. Shortly afterward Carol materialized at his side, oddly stark naked, no bodypaint, no cosmetics, only a tiny shapeless pair of flesh-tinted breasts. But she carried herself divinely. He couldn't resist gazing in open admiration. Carol smiled back and mouthed a greeting. He drew forth a chair and gestured at her to sit beside him. Garth tried to bound across the table but went limp in mid-air and fell in a heap beside Melody's chair.

"Garth is ill," Carol said, gazing straight across the table at Melody. "Something is wrong with him inside—it's all rotten."

"Can't they do anything for him?" David asked.

Carol shook her head, continuing to stare at Melody. "And you?" she said. "How have you been?"

"So-so," said Melody.

"But what have you been doing? What did you do last year?"

Melody shook her head. "I'm not supposed to tell you that."

"Why not?"

"Because he"—she pointed at David—"said I shouldn't."

Carol scowled and started to speak but David managed first:

"We went to Tibet."

"You shut up," Carol said. "I asked Melody."

"But—"

"No—I want Melody to tell me. Everybody knows how you feel. It's her I want to hear."

"He has to say I can," Melody said.

"Tell her," Carol commanded him.

"Talk," David said weakly.

"We went to Tibet," Melody said.

David groaned and dropped his chin to his chest. How could she fail to destroy him utterly?

"Lhasa?"

"No. Up. Way, way up. Into the mountains. The ones with the funny name. A shriveled bald monk lives up there. Brother Cupid. He's just like Christ and the others. You know."

"Yes," Carol said. "But what can he do?"

"Lots." Melody ticked off the wonders on the fingers of one hand. "He can show you heaven. And hell. He can show you the places that lie in between. And he can show you the meaning of life—its real significance." She shook her head. "He says that and—well—I guess he's right."

"So what is it?" Carol asked eagerly.

This is all wrong, David thought. Melody had forsaken the drama. All that remained was cold, crude fact. This time he had been destined for success and she had destroyed it for him.

But Melody was laughing. "You can't put something like that into words. If you could, then everybody would know."

"I see. But how—tell me—how did it affect you?"

Melody shook her head, leaning back. Shutting her eyes, tossing her head, she spoke without hesitation: "Nothing." Her eyes flew open. "It was just—just dull."

"No!" Carol cried.

"Yes," Melody said triumphantly. "That's exactly how it was. An utter, utter bore."

It was nearly twelve. David, who had waited until now, refused to remain silent a moment longer. Turning to Carol, he coldly demanded: "And what did you do last year?"

"Me?" Carol asked vaguely. Melody drew away from Carol's embrace and reached down to rouse Garth. David sat alone on the opposite side of the table.

"Yes, you," he said. "Who else?"

"I—I wouldn't know."

"You do have to tell us," Melody said. "We really have to know."

"But I . . ." Carol began.

"Yes?" said David.

"Well, nothing. I didn't do . . . anything."

"You liar!" he said.

"No. I—" She stood up, spreading her arms. "I really did nothing. We stayed home. I couldn't—"

"And how did you enjoy it?" Melody prodded. "Tell us that."

"I—we—" Carol hesitated. Her body stiffened. She stood straight up, balancing upon the tips of her toes, nearly leaving the floor, trembling as though striken by some awesome force from without. "It was wonderful!" she cried. "It was marvelous! Oh, David, I never knew before! I couldn't have guessed. It was so great—so grand!"

"No!" David shouted. He sprang to his feet.

"Oh, yes," Carol insisted, staring straight through him. "But you"—she laughed shrilly—"you'll never know."

Reaching out, she grabbed Melody warmly by the hand.

Here's another collaborative team, two young men from Texas who have both begun selling science fiction stories in the past few years. Together STEVEN UTLEY *and* HOWARD WALDROP *have produced a fascinating novelette of an alternative time-stream in which George Armstrong Custer lost his final battle to the Plains Indians Air Force—six fighter planes expertly piloted by such warriors as Crazy Horse and Black Man's Hand.*

For details on the battle and how it came about, see the following documents. (And if you should wonder how heavier-than-air craft could have been in military use as early as the Civil War, look carefully through the list of references at the end.)

Custer's Last Jump

BY STEVEN UTLEY & HOWARD WALDROP

Smithsonian Annals of Flight, VOL. 39: *The Air War in the West*
CHAPTER 27: The Krupp Monoplane

INTRODUCTION

Its wings still hold the tears from many bullets. The ailerons are still scorched black, and the exploded Henry machine rifle is bent awkwardly in its blast port.

The right landing skid is missing, and the frame has been restraightened. It stands in the left wing of the Air Museum today, next to the French Devre jet and the X-FU-5 Flying Flapjack, the world's fastest fighter aircraft.

On its rudder is the swastika, an ugly reminder of days of glory fifty years ago.

A simple plaque describes the aircraft. It reads:

CRAZY HORSE'S KRUPP MONOPLANE
(*Captured at the raid on Fort Carson, January 5, 1882*)

1. To study the history of this plane is to delve into one of
the most glorious eras of aviation history. To begin: the aircraft was manufactured by the Krupp plant at Haavesborg,
Netherlands. The airframe was completed August 3, 1862, as
part of the third shipment of Krupp aircraft to the Confederate States of America under terms of the Agreement of
Atlanta of 1861. It was originally equipped with power plant
⚒311 Zed of 87¼ horsepower, manufactured by the Jumo
plant at Nordmung, Duchy of Austria, on May 3 of the year
1862. Wingspan of the craft is twenty-three feet, its length is
seventeen feet three inches. The aircraft arrived in the port of
Charlotte on September 21, 1862, aboard the transport *Men-
denhall,* which had suffered heavy bombardment from GAR
picket ships. The aircraft was possibly sent by rail to Confederate Army Air Corps Center at Fort Andrew Mott, Alabama. Unfortunately, records of rail movements during this
time were lost in the burning of the Confederate archives at
Ittebeha in March 1867, two weeks after the Truce of Haldeman was signed.

2. The aircraft was damaged during a training flight in December 1862. Student pilot was Flight Subaltern (Cadet)
Neldoo J. Smith, CSAAC; flight instructor during the ill-fated
flight was Air Captain Winslow Homer Winslow, on interserv-
ice instructor-duty loan from the Confederate States Navy.

Accident forms and maintenance officer's reports indicate
that the original motor was replaced with one of the new 93½
horsepower Jumo engines which had just arrived from
Holland by way of Mexico.

3. The aircraft served routinely through the remainder of
Flight Subaltern Smith's training. We have records[141], which
indicate that the aircraft was one of the first to be equipped
with the Henry repeating machine rifle of the chain-driven
type. Until December 1862, all CSAAC aircraft were equipped

with the Sharps repeating rifles of the motor-driven, low-voltage type on wing or turret mounts.

As was the custom, the aircraft was flown by Flight Subaltern Smith to his first duty station at Thimblerig Aerodrome in Augusta, Georgia. Flight Subaltern Smith was assigned to Flight Platoon 2, 1st Aeroscout Squadron.

4. The aircraft, with Flight Subaltern Smith at the wheel, participated in three of the aerial expeditions against the Union Army in the Second Battle of the Manassas. Smith distinguished himself in the first and third mission. (He was assigned aerial picket duty south of the actual battle during his second mission.) On the first, he is credited with one kill and one probable (both bi-wing Airsharks). During the third mission, he destroyed one aircraft and forced another down behind Confederate lines. He then escorted the craft of his immediate commander, Air Captain Dalton Trump, to a safe landing on a field controlled by the Confederates. According to Trump's sworn testimony, Smith successfully fought off two Union craft and ranged ahead of Trump's crippled plane to strafe a group of Union soldiers who were in their flight path, discouraging them from firing on Trump's smoking aircraft.

For heroism on these two missions, Smith was awarded the Silver Star and Bar with Air Cluster. Presentation was made on March 3, 1863, by the late General J. E. B. Stuart, Chief of Staff of the CSAAC.

5. Flight Subaltern Smith was promoted to flight captain on April 12, 1863, after distinguishing himself with two kills and two probables during the first day of the Battle of the Three Roads, North Carolina. One of his kills was an airship of the Moby class, with crew of fourteen. Smith shared with only one other aviator the feat of bringing down one of these dirigibles during the War of the Secession.

This was the first action the 1st Aeroscout Squadron had seen since Second Manassas, and Captain Smith seems to have been chafing under inaction. Perhaps this led him to volunteer for duty with Major John S. Moseby, then forming

what would later become Moseby's Raiders. This was actually
sound military strategy: the CSAAC was to send a unit to
southwestern Kansas to carry out harassment raids against the
poorly defended forts of the far West. These raids would force
the Union to send men and materiel sorely needed at the
southern front far to the west, where they would be ineffectual
in the outcome of the war. That this action was taken is
pointed to by some[142] as a sign that the Confederate States
envisioned defeat and were resorting to desperate measures
four years before the Treaty of Haldeman.

At any rate, Captain Smith and his aircraft joined a triple
flight of six aircraft each, which, after stopping at El Dorado,
Arkansas, to refuel, flew away on a westerly course. This is
the last time they ever operated in Confederate states. The
date was June 5, 1863.

6.   The Union forts stretched from a medium-well-defended
line in Illinois, to poorly garrisoned stations as far west as
Wyoming Territory and south to the Kansas-Indian Territory
border. Southwestern Kansas was both sparsely settled and
garrisoned. It was from this area that Moseby's Raiders, with
the official designation 1st Western Interdiction Wing,
CSAAC, operated.

A supply wagon train had been sent ahead a month before
from Fort Worth, carrying petrol, ammunition, and material
for shelters. A crude landing field, hangars, and barracks
awaited the eighteen craft.

After two months of reconnaissance (done by mounted
scouts due to the need to maintain the element of surprise,
and, more importantly, by the limited amount of fuel available) the 1st WIW took to the air. The citizens of Riley, Kansas, long remembered the day: their first inkling that Confederates were closer than Texas came when motors were heard
overhead and the Union garrison was literally blown off the
face of the map.

7.   Following the first raid, word went to the War Department headquarters in New York, with pleas for aid and rein-

forcements for all Kansas garrisons. Thus the CSAAC achieved its goal in the very first raid. The effects snowballed; as soon as the populace learned of the raid, it demanded protection from nearby garrisons. Farmers' organizations threatened to stop shipments of needed produce to eastern depots. The garrison commanders, unable to promise adequate protection, appealed to higher military authorities.

Meanwhile, the 1st WIW made a second raid on Abilene, heavily damaging the railways and stockyards with twenty-five-pound fragmentation bombs. They then circled the city, strafed the Army Quartermaster depot, and disappeared into the west.

8.   This second raid, and the ensuing clamor from both the public and the commanders of western forces, convinced the War Department to divert new recruits and supplies, with seasoned members of the 18th Aeropursuit Squadron, to the Kansas-Missouri border, near Lawrence.

9.   Inclement weather in the fall kept both the 18th AS and the 1st WIW grounded for seventy-two of the ninety days of the season. Aircraft from each of these units met several times; the 1st is credited with one kill, while pilots of the 18th downed two Confederate aircraft on the afternoon of December 12, 1863.

Both aircraft units were heavily resupplied during this time. The Battle of the Canadian River was fought on December 18, when mounted reconnaissance units of the Union and Confederacy met in Indian territory. Losses were small on both sides, but the skirmish was the first of what would become known as the Far Western Campaign.

10.   Civilians spotted the massed formation of the 1st WIW as early as 10 A.M. Thursday, December 16, 1863. They headed northeast, making a leg due north when eighteen miles south of Lawrence. Two planes sped ahead to destroy the telegraph station at Felton, nine miles south of Lawrence. Nevertheless, a message of some sort reached Lawrence; a Union

messenger on horseback was on his way to the aerodrome
when the first flight of Confederate aircraft passed overhead.

In the ensuing raid, seven of the nineteen Union aircraft
were destroyed on the ground and two were destroyed in the
air, while the remaining aircraft were severely damaged and
the barracks and hangars demolished.

The 1st WIW suffered one loss: during the raid a Union
clerk attached for duty with the 18th AS manned an Agar
machine rifle position and destroyed one Confederate aircraft.
He was killed by machine rifle fire from the second wave of
planes. Private Alden Evans Gunn was awarded the Congres-
sional Medal of Honor posthumously for his gallantry during
the attack.

For the next two months, the 1st WIW ruled the skies as
far north as Illinois, as far east as Trenton, Missouri.

THE FAR WESTERN CAMPAIGN

1. At this juncture, the two most prominent figures of the
next nineteen years of frontier history enter the picture: the
Oglala Sioux Crazy Horse and Lieutenant Colonel (Brevet
Major General) George Armstrong Custer. The clerical error
giving Custer the rank of Brigadier General is well known. It
is not common knowledge that Custer was considered by the
General Staff as a candidate for Far Western Commander as
early as the spring of 1864, a duty he would not take up until
May 1869, when the Far Western Command was the only
theater of war operations within the Americas.

The General Staff, it is believed, considered Major General
Custer for the job for two reasons: they thought Custer possessed those qualities of spirit suited to the warfare necessary
in the Western Command, and that the far West was the ideal
place for the twenty-three-year-old Boy General.

Crazy Horse, the Oglala Sioux warrior, was with a hunting
party far from Oglala territory, checking the size of the few
remaining buffalo herds before they started their spring mi-
grations. Legend has it that Crazy Horse and the party were
crossing the prairies in early February 1864 when two air-

craft belonging to the 1st WIW passed nearby. Some of the Sioux jumped to the ground, believing that they were looking on the Thunderbird and its mate. Only Crazy Horse stayed on his pony and watched the aircraft disappear into the south.

He sent word back by the rest of the party that he and two of his young warrior friends had gone looking for the nest of the Thunderbird.

2. The story of the 1st WIW here becomes the story of the shaping of the Indian wars, rather than part of the history of the last four years of the War of the Secession. It is well known that increased alarm over the Kansas raids had shifted War Department thinking: the defense of the far West changed in importance from a minor matter in the larger scheme of war to a problem of vital concern. For one thing, the Confederacy was courting the Emperor Maximilian of Mexico, and through him the French, into entering the war on the Confederate side. The South wanted arms, but most necessarily to break the Union submarine blockade. Only the French Navy possessed the capability.

The Union therefore sent the massed 5th Cavalry to Kansas, and attached to it the 12th Air Destroyer Squadron and the 2nd Airship Command.

The 2nd Airship Command, at the time of its deployment, was equipped with the small pursuit airships known in later days as the "torpedo ship," from its double-pointed ends. These ships were used for reconnaissance and light interdiction duties, and were almost always accompanied by aircraft from the 12th ADS. They immediately set to work patrolling the Kansas skies from the renewed base of operations at Lawrence.

3. The idea of using Indian personnel in some phase of airfield operations in the West had been proposed by Moseby as early as June 1863. The C of C, CSA, disapproved in the strongest possible terms. It was not a new idea, therefore, when Crazy Horse and his two companions rode into the airfield, accompanied by the sentries who had challenged

them far from the perimeter. They were taken to Major Moseby for questioning.

Through an interpreter, Moseby learned they were Oglala, not Crows sent to spy for the Union. When asked why they had come so far, Crazy Horse replied, "To see the nest of the Thunderbird."

Moseby is said to have laughed[143] and then taken the three Sioux to see the aircraft. Crazy Horse was said to have been stricken with awe when he found that men controlled their flight.

Crazy Horse then offered Moseby ten ponies for one of the craft. Moseby explained that they were not his to give, but his Great Father's, and that they were used to fight the Yellowlegs from the Northeast.

At this time, fate took a hand: the 12th Air Destroyer Squadron had just begun operations. The same day Crazy Horse was having his initial interview with Moseby, a scout plane returned with the news that the 12th was being reinforced by an airship combat group; the dirigibles had been seen maneuvering near the Kansas-Missouri border.

Moseby learned from Crazy Horse that the warrior was respected; if not in his own tribe, then with other Nations of the North. Moseby, with an eye toward those reinforcements arriving in Lawrence, asked Crazy Horse if he could guarantee safe conduct through the northern tribes, and land for an airfield should the present one have to be abandoned.

Crazy Horse answered, "I can talk the idea to the People; it will be for them to decide."

Mosby told Crazy Horse that if he could secure the promise, he would grant him anything within his power.

Crazy Horse looked out the window toward the hangars. "I ask that you teach me and ten of my brother-friends to fly the Thunderbirds. We will help you fight the Yellowlegs."

Moseby, expecting requests for beef, blankets, or firearms was taken aback. Unlike the others who had dealt with the Indians, he was a man of his word. He told Crazy Horse he would ask his Great Father if this could be done. Crazy Horse

left, returning to his village in the middle of March. He and
several warriors traveled extensively that spring, smoking the
pipe, securing permissions from the other Nations for safe
conduct for the Gray White Men through their hunting lands.
His hardest task came in convincing the Oglala themselves
that the airfield be build in their southern hunting grounds.

Crazy Horse, his two wives, seven warriors and their
women, children, and belongings rode into the CSAAC airfield in June, 1864.

4. Moseby had been granted permission from Stuart to go
ahead with the training program. Derision first met the request within the southern General Staff when Moseby's proposal was circulated. Stuart, though not entirely sympathetic
to the idea, became its champion. Others objected, warning
that ignorant savages should not be given modern weapons.
Stuart reminded them that some of the good Tennessee boys
already flying airplanes could neither read nor write.

Stuart's approval arrived a month before Crazy Horse and
his band made camp on the edge of the airfield.

5. It fell to Captain Smith to train Crazy Horse. The Indian
became what Smith, in his journal,[144] describes as "the best
natural pilot I have seen or it has been my pleasure to fly
with." Part of this seems to have come from Smith's own mod-
esty; by all accounts, Smith was one of the finer pilots of the
war.

The operations of the 12th ADS and the 2nd Airship Command ranged closer to the CSAAC airfield. The dogfights
came frequently and the fighting grew less gentlemanly. One
1st WIW fighter was pounced by three aircraft of the 12th simultaneously: they did not stop firing even when the pilot signaled that he was hit and that his engine was dead. Nor did
they break off their runs until both pilot and craft plunged
into the Kansas prairie. It is thought that the Union pilots were
under secret orders to kill all members of the 1st WIW. There
is some evidence[145] that this rankled with the more gentle-

manly of the 12th Air Destroyer Squadron. Nevertheless, fighting intensified.

A flight of six more aircraft joined the 1st WIW some weeks after the Oglala Sioux started their training: this was the first of the ferry flights from Mexico through Texas and Indian territory to reach the airfield. Before the summer was over, a dozen additional craft would join the Wing; this before shipments were curtailed by Juarez's revolution against the French and the ouster and execution of Maximilian and his family.

Smith records[146] that Crazy Horse's first solo took place on August 14, 1864, and that the warrior, though deft in the air, still needed practice on his landings. He had a tendency to come in overpowered and to stall his engine out too soon. Minor repairs were made on the skids of the craft after this flight.

All this time, Crazy Horse had flown Smith's craft. Smith, after another week of hard practice with the Indian, pronounced him "more qualified than most pilots the CSAAC in Alabama turned out"[147] and signed over the aircraft to him. Crazy Horse begged off. Then, seeing that Smith was sincere, he gave the captain many buffalo hides. Smith reminded the Indian that the craft was not his: during their off hours, when not training, the Indians had been given enough instruction in military discipline as Moseby, never a stickler, thought necessary. The Indians had only a rudimentary idea of government property. Of the seven other Indian men, three were qualified as pilots; the other four were given gunner positions in the Krupp bi-wing light bombers assigned to the squadron.

Soon after Smith presented the aircraft to Crazy Horse, the captain took off in a borrowed monoplane on what was to be the daily weather flight into northern Kansas. There is evidence[148] that it was Smith who encountered a flight of light dirigibles from the 2nd Airship Command and attacked them single-handedly. He crippled one airship; the other was rescued when two escort planes of the 12th ADS came to its defense. They raked the attacker with withering fire. The attacker escaped into the clouds.

It was not until 1897, when a group of schoolchildren on an outing found the wreckage, that it was known that Captain Smith had brought his crippled monoplane within five miles of the airfield before crashing into the rolling hills.

When Smith did not return from his flight, Crazy Horse went on a vigil, neither sleeping nor eating for a week. On the seventh day, Crazy Horse vowed vengeance on the men who had killed his white friend.

6. The devastating Union raid of September 23, 1864, caught the airfield unawares. Though the Indians were averse to fighting at night, Crazy Horse and two other Sioux were manning three of the four craft which got off the ground during the raid. The attack had been carried out by the 2nd Airship Command, traveling at twelve thousand feet, dropping fifty-pound fragmentation bombs and shrapnel canisters. The shrapnel played havoc with the aircraft on the ground. It also destroyed the mess hall and enlisted barracks and three teepees.

The dirigibles turned away and were running fast before a tail wind when Crazy Horse gained their altitude.

The gunners on the dirigibles filled the skies with tracers from their light .30-30 machine rifles. Crazy Horse's monoplane was equipped with a single Henry .41-40 machine rifle. Unable to get in close killing distance, Crazy Horse and his companions stood off beyond range of the lighter Union guns and raked the dirigibles with heavy machine rifle fire. They did enough damage to force one airship down twenty miles from its base, and to ground two others for two days while repairs were made. The intensity of fire convinced the airship commanders that more than four planes had made it off the ground, causing them to continue their headlong retreat.

Crazy Horse and the others returned, and brought off the second windfall of the night; a group of 5th Cavalry raiders

were to have attacked the airfield in the confusion of the airship raid and burn everything still standing. On their return
flight, the four craft encountered the cavalry unit as it began
its charge across open ground.

In three strafing runs, the aircraft killed thirty-seven men
and wounded fifty-three, while twenty-nine were taken prisoner by the airfield's defenders. Thus, in his first combat mission for the CSAAC, Crazy Horse was credited with saving
the airfield against overwhelming odds.

7.   Meanwhile, Major General George A. Custer had distinguished himself at the Battle of Gettysburg. A few weeks after
the battle, he enrolled himself in the GAR jump school at Wa-
tauga, New York. Howls of outrage came from the General
Staff; Custer quoted the standing order, "any man who volunteered and of whom the commanding officer approved," could
be enrolled. Custer then asked, in a letter to C of S, GAR,
"how any military leader could be expected to plan maneu-
vers involving parachute infantry when he himself had never
experienced a drop, or found the true capabilities of the parachute infantryman?"[149] The Chief of Staff shouted down the
protest. There were mutterings among the General Staff[150]
to the effect that the real reason Custer wanted to become
jump-qualified was so that he would have a better chance of
leading the Invasion of Atlanta, part of whose contingency
plans called for attacks by airborne units.

During the three-week parachute course, Custer became
acquainted with another man who would play an important
part in the Western Campaign, Captain (Brevet Colonel)
Frederick W. Benteen. Upon graduation from the jump
school, Brevet Colonel Benteen assumed command of the
505th Balloon Infantry, stationed at Chicago, Illinois, for
training purposes. Colonel Benteen would remain commander
of the 505th until his capture at the Battle of Montgomery in
1866. While he was prisoner of war, his command was given
to another, later to figure in the Western Campaign, Lieutenant Colonel Myles W. Keogh.

Custer, upon successful completion of jump school, returned to his command of the 6th Cavalry Division, and participated throughout the remainder of the war in that capacity. It was he who led the successful charge at the Battle of the Cape Fear which smashed Lee's flank and allowed the 1st Infantry to overrun the Confederate position and capture that southern leader. Custer distinguished himself and his command up until the cessation of hostilities in 1867.

8. The 1st WIW, CSAAC, moved to a new airfield in Wyoming Territory three weeks after the raid of September 24. At the same time, the 2nd WIW was formed and moved to an outpost in Indian territory. The 2nd WIW raided the Union airfield, took it totally by surprise, and inflicted casualties on the 12th ADS and 2nd AC so devastating as to render them ineffectual. The 2nd WIW then moved to a second field in Wyoming Territory. It was here, following the move, that a number of Indians, including Black Man's Hand, were trained by Crazy Horse.

9. We leave the history of the 2nd WIW here. It was redeployed for the defense of Montgomery. The Indians and aircraft in which they trained were sent north to join the 1st WIW. The 1st WIW patrolled the skies of Indiana, Nebraska, and the Dakotas. After the defeat of the 12th ADS and the 2nd AC, the Union forstalled attempts to retaliate until the cessation of southern hostilities in 1867.

We may at this point add that Crazy Hose, Black Man's Hand, and the other Indians sometimes left the airfield during periods of long inactivity. They returned to their Nations for as long as three months at a time. Each time Crazy Horse returned, he brought one or two pilot or gunner recruits with him. Before the winter of 1866, more than thirty per cent of the 1st WIW were Oglala, Sansarc Sioux, or Cheyenne.

The South, losing the war of attrition, diverted all supplies to Alabama and Mississippi in the fall of 1866. None were forthcoming for the 1st WIW, though a messenger arrived with orders for Major Moseby to return to Texas for the defense of Fort Worth, where he would later direct the Battle of the Trinity. That Moseby was not ordered to deploy the 1st

WIW to that defense has been considered by many military
strategists as a "lost turning point" of the battle for Texas.
Command of the 1st WIW was turned over to Acting Major
(Flight Captain) Natchitoches Hooley.

10.   The loss of Moseby signaled the end of the 1st WIW.
Not only did the nondeployment of the 1st to Texas cost the
South that territory, it also left the 1st in an untenable position, which the Union was quick to realize. The airfield was
captured in May 1867 by a force of five hundred cavalry and
three hundred infantry sent from the battle of the Arkansas,
and a like force, plus aircraft, from Chicago. Crazy Horse,
seven Indians, and at least five Confederates escaped in their
monoplanes. The victorious Union troops were surprised to
find Indians at the field. Crazy Horse's people were eventually
freed; the Army thought them to have been hired by the Confederates to hunt and cook for the airfield. Moseby had provided for this in contingency plans long before; he had not
wanted the Plains tribes to suffer for Confederate acts. The
Army did not know, and no one volunteered the information,
that it had been Indians doing the most considerable amount
of damage to the Union garrisons lately.

   Crazy Horse and three of his Indians landed their craft near
the Black Hills. The Cheyenne helped them carry the craft, on
travois, to caves in the sacred mountains. Here they moth-
balled the planes with mixtures of pine tar and resins, and
sealed up the caves.

11.   The aircraft remained stored until February 1872. During this time, Crazy Horse and his Oglala Sioux operated, like
the other Plains Indians, as light cavalry, skirmishing with the
Army and with settlers up and down the Dakotas and Montana. George Armstrong Custer was appointed commander of
the new 7th Cavalry in 1869. Stationed first at Chicago (Far
Western Command headquarters) they later moved to Fort
Abraham Lincoln, Nebraska.

   A column of troops moved against Indians on the warpath
in the winter of 1869. They reported a large group of Indians

encamped on the Washita River. Custer obtained permission
for the 505th Balloon Infantry to join the 7th Cavalry. From
that day on, the unit was officially Company I (Separate
Troops), 7th U. S. Cavalry, though it kept its numerical designation. Also attached to the 7th was the 12th Airship
Squadron, as Company J.

Lieutenant Colonel Keogh, acting commander of the 505th
for the last twenty-one months, but who had never been on
jump status, was appointed by Custer as commander of K
Company, 7th Cavalry.

It was known that only the 505th Balloon Infantry and the
12th Airship Squadron were used in the raid on Black Kettle's
village. Black Kettle was a treaty Indian, "walking the white
man's road." Reports have become garbled in transmission:
Custer and the 505th believed they were jumping into a village of hostiles.

The event remained a mystery until Kellogg, the Chicago
newspaperman, wrote his account in 1872.[151] The 505th, with
Custer in command, flew the three (then numbered, after
1872, named) dirigibles No. 31, No. 76, and No. 93, with
seventy-two jumpers each. Custer was in the first "stick" on
Airship 76. The three sailed silently to the sleeping village.
Custer gave the order to hook up at 5:42 Chicago time, 4:42
local time, and the 505th jumped into the village. Black Kettle's people were awakened when some of the balloon infantry
crashed through their teepees, others died in their sleep. One
of the first duties of the infantry was to moor the dirigibles;
this done, the gunners on the airships opened up on the startled villagers with their Gatling and Agar machine rifles.
Black Kettle himself was killed while waving an American
flag at Airship No. 93.

After the battle, the men of the 505th climbed back up to
the moored dirigibles by rope ladder, and the airships de-
parted for Fort Lincoln. The Indians camped downriver
heard the shooting and found horses stampeded during the attack. When they came to the village, they found only slaughter. Custer had taken his dead (3, one of whom died during

the jump by being drowned in the Washita) and wounded
(12) away. They left 307 dead men, women, and children,
and 500 slaughtered horses.

There were no tracks leading in and out of the village
except those of the frightened horses. The other Indians left
the area, thinking the white men had magicked it.

Crazy Horse is said[152] to have visited the area soon after the
massacre. It was this action by the 7th which spelled their
doom seven years later.

12.   Black Man's Hand joined Crazy Horse; so did other former 1st WIW pilots, soon after Crazy Horse's two-plane raid
on the airship hangars at Bismark, in 1872. For that mission,
Crazy Horse dropped twenty-five-pound fragmentation bombs
tied to petrol canisters. The shrapnel ripped the dirigibles, the
escaping hydrogen was ignited by the burning petrol: all—
hangars, balloons, and maintenance crews—were lost.

It was written up as an unreconstructed Confederate's sabotage; a somewhat ignominious former southern major was
eventually hanged on circumstantial evidence. Reports by
sentries that they heard aircraft just before the explosions
were discounted. At the time, it was believed the only aircraft
were those belonging to the Army, and the carefully licensed
commercial craft.

13.   In 1874, Custer circulated rumors that the Black Hills
were full of gold. It has been speculated that this was used to
draw miners to the area so the Indians would attack them;
then the cavalry would have unlimited freedom to deal with
the Red Man.[153] Also that year, those who had become
Agency Indians were being shorted in their supplies by
members of the scandal-plagued Indian Affairs Bureau under
President Grant. When these left the reservations in search of
food, the cavalry was sent to "bring them back." Those who
were caught were usually killed.

The Sioux ignored the miners at first, expecting the gods to
deal with them. When this did not happen, Sitting Bull sent
out a party of two hundred warriors, who killed every miner

they encountered. Public outrage demanded reprisals; Sheridan wired Custer to find and punish those responsible.

14.   Fearing what was to come, Crazy Horse sent Yellow Dog and Red Chief with a war party of five hundred to raid the rebuilt Fort Phil Kearny. This they did successfully, capturing twelve planes and fuel and ammunition for many more. They hid these in the caverns with the 1st WIW craft.

The Army would not have acted as rashly as it did had it known the planes pronounced missing in the reports on the Kearny raid were being given into the hands of experienced pilots.

The reprisal consisted of airship patrols which strafed any living thing on the plains. Untold thousands of deer and the few remaining buffalo were killed. Unofficial counts list as killed a little more than eight hundred Indians who were caught in the open during the next eight months.

Indians who jumped the agencies and who had seen or heard of the slaughter streamed to Sitting Bull's hidden camp on the Little Big Horn. They were treated as guests, except for the Sansarcs, who camped a little way down the river. It is estimated there were no less than ten thousand Indians, including some four thousand warriors, camped along the river for the Sun Dance ceremony of June 1876.

A three-pronged-pincers movement for the final eradication of the Sioux and Cheyenne worked toward them. The 7th Cavalry, under Keogh and Major Marcus Reno, set out from Fort Lincoln during the last week of May. General George Crook's command was coming up the Rosebud. The gunboat *Far West,* with three hundred reserves and supplies, steamed to the mouth of the Big Horn River. General Terry's command was coming from the northwest. All Indians they encountered were to be killed.

Just before the Sun Dance, Crazy Horse and his pilots got word of the movement of Crook's men up the Rosebud, hurried to the caves, and prepared their craft for flight. Only six planes were put in working condition in time. The other pilots remained behind while Crazy Horse, Black Man's Hand, and four others took to the skies. They destroyed two dirigibles, soundly trounced Crook, and chased his command back down the Rosebud in a rout. The column had to abandon their light armored vehicles and fight its way back, on foot for the most part, to safety.

15. Sitting Bull's vision during the Sun Dance is well known.[154] He told it to Crazy Horse, the warrior who would see that it came true, as soon as the aviators returned to camp.

Two hundred fifty miles away, "Chutes and Saddles" was sounded on the morning of June 23, and the men of the 505th Balloon Infantry climbed aboard the airships *Benjamin Franklin, Samuel Adams, John Hancock,* and *Ethan Allen.* Custer was first man on stick one of the *Franklin.* The *Ethan Allen* carried a scout aircraft which could hook up or detach in flight; the bi-winger was to serve as liaison between the three armies and the airships.

When Custer bade goodbye to his wife, Elizabeth, that morning, both were in good spirits. If either had an inkling of the fate which awaited Custer and the 7th three days away, on the bluffs above a small stream, they did not show it.

The four airships sailed from Fort Lincoln, their silver sides and shark-tooth mouths gleaming in the sun, the eyes painted on the noses looking west. On the sides were the crossed sabers of the cavalry; above the numeral 7; below the numerals 505. It is said that they looked magnificent as they sailed away for their rendezvous with destiny.[155]

16. It is sufficient to say that the Indians attained their greatest victory over the Army, and almost totally destroyed the 7th Cavalry, on June 25–26, 1876, due in large part to the efforts of Crazy Horse and his aviators. Surprise, swiftness, and the skill of the Indians cannot be discounted, nor can the military blunders made by Custer that morning. The repercussions of that summer day rang down the years, and the events are still debated. The only sure fact is that the U. S.

Army lost its prestige, part of its spirit, and more than four hundred of its finest soldiers in the battle.

17. While the demoralized commands were sorting themselves out, the Cheyenne and Sioux left for the Canadian border. They took their aircraft with them, on travois. With Sitting Bull, Crazy Horse and his band settled just across the border. The aircraft were rarely used again until the attack on the camp by the combined Canadian-U. S. Cavalry offensive of 1879. Crazy Horse and his aviators, as they had done so many times before, escaped with their aircraft, using one of the planes to carry their remaining fuel. Two of the nine craft were shot down by a Canadian battery.

Crazy Horse, sensing the end, fought his way, with men on horseback and the planes on travois, from Montana to Colorado. After learning of the death of Sitting Bull and Chief Joseph, he took his small band as close as he dared to Fort Carson, where the cavalry was amassing to wipe out the remaining American Indians.

He assembled his men for the last time. He made his proposal; all concurred and joined him for a last raid on the Army. The five remaining planes came in low, the morning of January 5, 1882, toward the Army airfield. They destroyed twelve aircraft on the ground, shot up the hangars and barracks, and ignited one of the two ammunition dumps of the stockade. At this time, Army gunners manned the William's machine cannon batteries (improved by Thomas Edison's contract scientists) and blew three of the craft to flinders. The war gods must have smiled on Crazy Horse; his aircraft was crippled, the machine rifle was blown askew, the motor slivered, but he managed to set down intact. Black Man's Hand turned away; he was captured two months later, eating cottonwood bark in the snows of Arizona.

Crazy Horse jumped from his aircraft as most of Fort Carson ran toward him; he pulled two Sharps repeating carbines from the cockpit and blazed away at the astonished troopers, wounding six and killing one. His back to the craft, he contin-

ued to fire until more than one hundred infantrymen fired a
volley into his body.

The airplane was displayed for seven months at Fort Carson before being sent to the Smithsonian in Pittsburgh, where
it stands today. Thus passed an era of military aviation.

—LT. GEN. FRANK LUKE, JR.
USAF, Ret.

From the December 2, 1939, issue of *Collier's Magazine*
Custer's Last Jump?
BY A. R. REDMOND

Few events in American history have captured the imagination so thoroughly as the Battle of the Little Big Horn. Lieutenant Colonel George Armstrong Custer's devastating defeat
at the hands of Sioux and Cheyenne Indians in June 1876 has
been rendered time and again by such celebrated artists as
George Russell and Frederic Remington. Books, factual and
otherwise, which have been written around or about the battle
would fill an entire library wing. The motion picture industry
has on numerous occasions drawn upon "Custer's Last Jump"
for inspiration; latest in a long line of movieland Custers is
Erroll Flynn [see photo], who appears with Olivia
deHavilland and newcomer Anthony Quinn in Warner
Brother's soon-to-be-released *They Died With Their Chutes
On.*

The impetuous and flamboyant Custer was an almost leg-
endary figure long before the Battle of the Little Big Horn,
however. Appointed to West Point in 1857, Custer was
placed in command of Troop G, 2nd Cavalry, in June 1861,
and participated in a series of skirmishes with Confederate
cavalry throughout the rest of the year. It was during the First
Battle of Manassas, or Bull Run, that he distinguished himself. He continued to do so in other engagements—at
Williamsburg, Chancellorsville, Gettysburg—and rose rapidly

through the ranks. He was twenty-six years old when he received a promotion to Brigadier General. He was, of course, immediately dubbed the Boy General. He had become an authentic war hero when the Northerners were in dire need of nothing less during those discouraging months between First Manassas and Gettysburg.

With the cessation of hostilities in the East when Bragg surrendered to Grant at Haldeman, the small hamlet about eight miles from Morehead, Kentucky, Custer requested a transfer of command. He and his young bride wound up at Chicago, manned by the new 7th U. S. Cavalry.

The war in the West lasted another few months; the tattered remnants of the Confederate Army staged last desperate stands throughout Texas, Colorado, Kansas, and Missouri. The final struggle at the Trinity River in October 1867 marked the close of conflict between North and South. Those few Mexican military advisers left in Texas quietly withdrew across the Rio Grande. The French, driven from Mexico in 1864 when Maximilian was ousted, lost interest in the Americas when they became embroiled with the newly united Prussian states.

During his first year in Chicago, Custer familiarized himself with the airships and aeroplanes of the 7th. The only jump-qualified general officer of the war, Custer seemed to have felt no resentment at the ultimate fate of mounted troops boded by the extremely mobile flying machines. The Ohio-born Boy General eventually preferred traveling aboard the airship *Benjamin Franklin,* one of the eight craft assigned to the 505th Balloon Infantry (Troop I, 7th Cavalry, commanded by Brevet Colonel Frederick Benteen) while his horse soldiers rode behind the very capable Captain (Brevet Lt. Col.) Myles Keogh.

The War Department in Pittsburgh did not know that various members of the Plains Indian tribes had been equipped with aeroplanes by the Confederates, and that many had actually flown against the Union garrisons in the West. (Curiously enough, those tribes which held out the longest against the

Army—most notably the Apaches under Geronimo in the deep Southwest—were those who did not have aircraft.) The problems of transporting and hiding, to say nothing of maintaining planes, outweighed the advantages. A Cheyenne warrior named Brave Bear is said to have traded his band's aircraft in disgust to Sitting Bull for three horses. Also, many of the Plains Indians hated the aircraft outright, as they had been used by the white men to decimate the great buffalo herds in the early 1860s.

Even so, certain Oglalas, Minneconjous, and Cheyenne did reasonably well in the aircraft given them by the C. S. Army Air Corps Major John S. Moseby, whom the Indians called "The Gray White Man" or "Many-Feathers-in-Hat." The Oglala war chief Crazy Horse [see photo, overleaf] led the raid on the Bismarck hangars (1872), four months after the 7th Cavalry was transferred to Fort Abraham Lincoln, Dakota Territory, and made his presence felt at the Rosebud and Little Big Horn in 1876. The Cheyenne Black Man's Hand, trained by Crazy Horse himself, shot down two Army machines at the Rosebud, and was in the flight of planes that accomplished the annihilation of the 505th Balloon Infantry during the first phase of the Little Big Horn fiasco.

After the leveling of Fort Phil Kearny in February 1869, Custer was ordered to enter the Indian territories and punish those who had sought sanctuary there after the raid. Taking with him 150 parachutists aboard three airships, Custer left on the trail of a large band of Cheyenne.

On the afternoon of February 25, Lieutenant William van W. Reily, dispatched for scouting purposes in a Studebaker bi-winger, returned to report that he had shot up a hunting party near the Washita River. The Cheyenne, he thought, were encamped on the banks of the river some twenty miles away. They appeared not to have seen the close approach of the 7th Cavalry as they had not broken camp.

Just before dawn the next morning, the 505th Balloon Infantry, led by Custer, jumped into the village, killing all inhabitants and their animals.

For the next five years, Custer and the 7th chased the hostiles of the Plains back and forth between Colorado and the Canadian border. Relocated at Fort Lincoln, Custer and an expedition of horse soldiers, geologists, and engineers discovered gold in the Black Hills. Though the Black Hills still belonged to the Sioux according to several treaties, prospectors began to pour into the area. The 7th was ordered to protect them. The Blackfeet, Minneconjous, and Hunkpapa—Sioux who had left the warpath on the promise that the Black Hills, their sacred lands, was theirs to keep for all time—protested, and when protests brought no results, took matters into their own hands. Prospectors turned up in various stages of mutilation, or not at all.

Conditions worsened over the remainder of 1875, during which time the United States Government ordered the Sioux out of the Black Hills. To make sure the Indians complied, airships patrolled the skies of Dakota Territory.

By the end of 1875, plagued by the likes of Crazy Horse's Oglala Sioux, it was decided that there was but one solution to the Plains Indian problem—total extermination.

At this point, General Phil Sheridan, Commander in Chief of the United States Army, began working on the practical angle of this new policy toward the Red Man.

In January 1876, delegates from the Democratic Party approached George Armstrong Custer at Fort Abraham Lincoln and offered him the party's presidential nomination on the condition that he pull off a flashy victory over the red men before the national convention in Chicago in July.

On February 19, 1876, the Boy General's brother Thomas, commander of Troop C of the 7th, climbed into the observer's cockpit behind Lieutenant James C. Sturgis and took off on a routine patrol. Their aeroplane, a Whitney pusher-type, did not return. Ten days later its wreckage was found sixty miles west of Fort Lincoln. Apparently, Sturgis and Tom Custer had stumbled on a party of mounted hostiles and, swooping low to fire or drop a handbomb, suffered a lucky hit from one of the Indians' firearms. The mutilated remains of the two officers were found a quarter mile from the wreckage, indicating that they had escaped on foot after the crash but were caught.

The shock of his brother's death, combined with the Democrat's offer, were to lead Lieutenant Colonel G. A. Custer into the worst defeat suffered by an officer of the United States Army.

Throughout the first part of 1876, Indians drifted into Wyoming Territory from the east and south, driven by mounting pressure from the Army. Raids on small Indian villages had been stepped up. Waning herds of buffalo were being systematically strafed by the airships. General Phil Sheridan received reports of tribes gathering in the vicinity of the Wolf Mountains, in what is now southern Montana, and devised a strategy by which the hostiles would be crushed for all time.

Three columns were to converge upon the amassed Indians from the north, south, and east, the west being blocked by the Wolf Mountains. General George Crook's dirigibles, light tanks, and infantry were to come up the Rosebud River. General Alfred Terry would push from the northeast with infantry, cavalry, and field artillery. The 7th Cavalry was to move from the east. The Indians could not escape.

Commanded by Captain Keogh, Troops A, C, D, E, F, G, and H of the 7th—about 580 men, not counting civilian teamsters, interpreters, Crow and Arikara scouts—set out from Fort Lincoln five weeks ahead of the July 1 rendezvous at the junction of the Big Horn and Little Big Horn rivers. A month later, Custer and 150 balloon infantrymen aboard the airships *Franklin, Adams, Hancock,* and *Allen* set out on Keogh's trail.

Everything went wrong from that point onward.

The early summer of 1876 had been particularly hot and dry in Wyoming Territory. Crook, proceeding up the Rosebud, was slowed by the tanks, which theoretically traveled at five miles per hour but which kept breaking down from the heat and from the alkaline dust which worked its way into the engines through chinks in the three-inch armor plate. The crews roasted. On June 13, as Crook's column halted beside the Rosebud to let the tanks cool off, six monoplanes dived out of the clouds to attack the escorting airships *Paul Revere* and *John Paul Jones*. Caught by surprise, the two dirigibles were blown up and fell about five miles from Crook's position. The infantrymen watched, astonished, as the Indian aeronauts turned their craft toward them. While the foot soldiers ran for cover, several hundred mounted Sioux warriors showed up. In the ensuing rout, Crook lost forty-seven men and all his armored vehicles. He was still in headlong retreat when the Indians broke off their chase at nightfall.

The 7th Cavalry and the 505th Balloon Infantry linked up by liaison craft carried by the *Ethan Allen* some miles southeast of the hostile camp on the Little Big Horn on the evening of June 24. Neither they, nor Terry's column, had received word of Crook's retreat, but Keogh's scouts had sighted a large village ahead.

Custer did not know that this village contained not the five or six hundred Indians expected, but between eight and ten *thousand*, of whom slightly less than half were warriors. Spurred by his desire for revenge for his brother Tom, and filled with glory at the thought of the Democratic presidential nomination, Custer decided to hit the Indians before either Crook's or Terry's columns could reach the village. He settled on a scaled-down version of Sheridan's tri-pronged movement, and dispatched Keogh to the south, Reno to the east, with himself and the 505th attacking from the north. A small column was to wait downriver with the pack train. On the evening of June 24, George Armstrong Custer waited, secure in the knowledge that he, personally, would deal the Plains Indians their mortal blow within a mere twenty-four hours.

Unfortunately, the Indians amassed on the banks of the Little Big Horn—Oglalas, Minneconjous, Araphao, Hunkpapas, Blackfeet, Cheyenne, and so forth—had the idea that white men were on the way. During the Sun Dance Ceremony the week before, the Hunkpapa chief Sitting Bull had had a dream about soldiers falling into his camp. The hostiles, assured of victory, waited.

On the morning of June 25, the *Benjamin Franklin, Samuel Adams, John Hancock*, and *Ethan Allen* drifted quietly over the hills toward the village. They were looping south when the Indians attacked.

Struck by several spin-stabilized rockets, the *Samuel Adams* blew up with a flash that might have been seen by the officers and men riding behind Captain Keogh up the valley of the Little Big Horn. Eight or twelve Indians had, in the gray dawn, climbed for altitude above the ships.

Still several miles short of their intended drop zone, the balloon infantrymen piled out of the burning and exploding craft. Though each ship was armed with two Gatling rifles fore and aft, the airships were helpless against the airplanes' bullets and rockets. Approximately one hundred men, Custer included, cleared the ships. The Indian aviators made passes through them, no doubt killing several in the air. The *Franklin* and *Hancock* burned and fell to the earth across the river from the village. The *Allen*, dumping water ballast to gain altitude, turned for the Wolf Mountains. Though riddled by machine rifle fire, it did not explode and settled to earth about fifteen miles from where now raged a full-scale battle between increasingly demoralized soldiers and battle-maddened Sioux and Cheyenne.

Major Reno had charged the opposite side of the village as soon as he heard the commotion. Wrote one of his officers later: "A solid wall of Indians came out of the haze which had hidden the village from our eyes. They must have outnumbered us ten to one, and they were ready for us. . . . Fully a third of the column was down in three minutes."

Reno, fearing he would be swallowed up, pulled his men back across the river and took up a position in a stand of timber on the riverward slope of the knoll. The Indians left a few hundred braves to make certain Reno did not escape and moved off to Reno's right to descend on Keogh's flank.

The hundred-odd parachute infantrymen who made good their escape from the airship were scattered over three square miles. The ravines and gullies cutting up the hills around the village quickly filled with mounted Indians who rode through unimpeded by the random fire of disorganized balloon infantrymen. They swept them up, on the way to Keogh. Keogh, unaware of the number of Indians and the rout of Reno's command, got as far as the north bank of the river before he was ground to pieces between two masses of hostiles. Of Keogh's command, less than a dozen escaped the slaughter. The actual battle lasted about thirty minutes.

The hostiles left the area that night, exhausted after their greatest victory over the soldiers. Most of the Indians went north to Canada; some escaped the mass extermination of their race which was to take place in the American West during the next six years.

Terry found Reno entrenched on the ridge the morning of the twenty-seventh. The scouts sent to find Custer and Keogh could not believe their eyes when they found the bodies of the 7th Cavalry six miles away.

Some of the men were not found for another two days, Terry and his men scoured the ravines and valleys. Custer himself was about four miles from the site of Keogh's annihilation; the Boy General appears to have been hit by a piece of exploding rocket shrapnel and may have been dead before he reached the ground. His body escaped the mutilation that befell most of Keogh's command, possibly because of its distance from the camp.

Custer's miscalculation cost the Army 430 men, four dirigibles (plus the Studebaker scout from the *Ethan Allen*), and its prestige. An attempt was made to make a scapegoat of Major Reno, blaming his alleged cowardice for the failure of the 7th. Though Reno was acquitted, grumblings continued up until the turn of the century. It is hoped the matter will

be settled for all time by the opening, for private research, of
the papers of the late President Phil Sheridan. As Commander
in Chief, he had access to a mountain of material which was
kept from the public at the time of the court of inquiry in
1879.

Extract from *Huckleberry Among the Hostiles: A Journal*
BY MARK TWAIN, EDITED BY BERNARD VAN DYNE
Hutton and Company, New York, 1932.

EDITOR'S NOTE: In November 1886 Clemens drafted a ten-
tative outline for a sequel to *The Adventures of Huckleberry
Finn,* which had received mixed reviews on its publication in
January 1885, but which had nonetheless enjoyed a second
printing within five months of its release. The proposed sequel
was intended to deal with Huckleberry's adventures as a
young man on the frontier. To gather research material
firsthand, Mark boarded the airship *Peyton* in Cincinnati,
Ohio, in mid-December 1886, and set out across the Southwest, amassing copious notes and reams of interviews with
soldiers, frontiersmen, law enforcement officers, ex-hostiles, at
least two notorious outlaws, and a number of less readily cate-
gorized persons. Twain had intended to spend four months
out West. Unfortunately, his wife, Livy, fell gravely ill in late
February 1887; Twain returned to her as soon as he received
word in Fort Hood, Texas. He lost interest in all writing for
two years after her death in April 1887. The proposed novel
about Huckleberry Finn as a man was never written: we are
left with 110,000 words of interviews and observations, and
an incomplete journal of the author's second trek across the
American West.—BvD

Feb. 2:   A more desolate place than the Indian Territory
of Oklahoma would be impossible to imagine. It is flat the
year 'round, stingingly cold in winter, hot and dry, I am told,

during the summer (when the land turns brown save for scattered patches of greenery which serve only to make the landscape all the drearier; Arizona and New Mexico are devoid of greenery, which is to their credit—when those territories elected to become barren wastelands they did not lose heart halfway, but followed their chosen course to the end).

It is easy to see why the United States Government swept the few Indians into God-forsaken Oklahoma, and ordered them to remain there under threat of extermination. The word "God-forsaken" is the vital clue. The white men who "gave" this land to the few remaining tribes for as long as the wind shall blow—which it certainly does in February—and the grass shall grow (which it does, in Missouri, perhaps) were Christians who knew better than to let heathen savages run loose in parts of the country still smiled upon by our heavenly malefactor.

February 4: Whatever I may have observed about Oklahoma from the cabin of the *Peyton* has been reinforced by a view from the ground. The airship was running into stiff winds from the north, so we put in at Fort Sill yesterday evening and are awaiting calmer weather. I have gone on with my work.

Fort Sill is located seventeen miles from the Cheyenne Indian reservation. It has taken me all of a day to learn (mainly from one Sergeant Howard, a gap-toothed, unwashed Texan who is apparently my unofficial guardian angel for whatever length of time I am to be marooned here) that the Cheyenne do not care much for Oklahoma, which is still another reason why the government keeps them there. One or two ex-hostiles will leave the reservation every month, taking with them their wives and meager belongings, and Major Rickards will have to send out a detachment of soldiers to haul the erring ones back, either in chains or over the backs of horses. I am told the reservation becomes particularly annoying in the winter months, as the poor boys who are detailed to pursue the Indians suffer greatly from the cold. At this, I remarked to Sergeant Howard that the red man can be terribly inconsiderate, even ungrateful, in view of all the blessings the white man has heaped upon him—smallpox, and that French disease, to name two. The good sergeant scratched his head and grinned, and said, "You're right, sir."

I'll have to make Howard a character in the book.

February 5: Today, I was taken by Major Rickards to meet a Cheyenne named Black Man's Hand, one of the participants of the alleged massacre of the 7th Cavalry at the Little Big Horn River in '76. The major had this one Cheyenne brought in after a recent departure from the reservation. Black Man's Hand had been shackled and left to dwell upon his past misdeeds in an unheated hut at the edge of the airport, while two cold-benumbed privates stood on guard before the door. It was evidently feared this one savage would, if left unchained, do to Fort Sill that which he (with a modicum of assistance from four or five thousand of his race) had done to Custer. I nevertheless mentioned to Rickards that I was interested in talking to Black Man's Hand, as the Battle of the Little Big Horn would perfectly climax Huckleberry's adventures in the new book. Rickards was reluctant to grant permission but gave in abruptly, perhaps fearing I would model a villain after him.

Upon entering the hut where the Cheyenne sat, I asked Major Rickards if it were possible to have the Indian's manacles removed, as it makes me nervous to talk to a man who can rattle his chains at me whenever he chooses. Major Rickards said no and troubled himself to explain to me the need for limiting the movement of this specimen of ferocity within the walls of Fort Sill.

With a sigh, I seated myself across from Black Man's Hand and offered him one of my cigars. He accepted it with a faint smile. He appeared to be in his forties, though his face was deeply lined.

He was dressed in ragged leather leggings, thick calf-length woolen pajamas, and a faded Army jacket. His vest appears to have been fashioned from an old parachute harness. He had no hat, no footgear, and no blanket.

"Major Rickards," I said, "this man is freezing to death. Even if he isn't, I am. Can you provide this hut with a little warmth?"

The fretting major summarily dispatched one of the sentries for firewood and kindling for the little stove sitting uselessly in the corner of the hut.

I would have been altogether comfortable after that could I have had a decanter of brandy with which to force out the inner chill. But Indians are notoriously incapable of holding liquor, and I did not wish to be the cause of this poor wretch's further downfall.

Black Man's Hand speaks surprisingly good English. I spent an hour and a half with him, recording his remarks with as much attention paid to accuracy as my advanced years and cold fingers permitted. With luck, I'll be able to fill some gaps in his story before the *Peyton* resumes its flight across this griddlecake countryside.

Extract from *The Testament of Black Man's Hand*

[NOTE: for the sake of easier reading, I have substituted a number of English terms for these provided by the Cheyenne Black Man's Hand.—MT]

I was young when I first met the Oglala mystic Crazy Horse, and was taught by him to fly the Thunderbirds which the one called the Gray White Man had given him. [The Gray White Man—John S. Moseby, Major, CSAAC—MT] Some of the older men among the People [as the Cheyenne call themselves, Major Rickards explains; I assured him that such egocentricity is by no means restricted to savages—MT] did not think much of the flying machines and said, "How will we be able to remain brave men when this would enable us to fly over the heads of our enemies, without counting coup or taking trophies?"

But the Oglala said, "The Gray White Man has asked us to help him."

"Why should we help him?" asked Two Pines.

"Because he fights the blueshirts and those who persecute us. We have known for many years that the men who cheated us and lied to us and killed our women and the buffalo are men without honor, cowards who fight only because there is no other way for them to get what they want. They cannot understand why we fight with the Crows and Pawnees—to be brave, to win honor for ourselves. They fight because it is a means to an end, and they fight us only because we have what they want. The blueshirts want to kill us all. They fight to win. If we are to fight them, we must fight with their own weapons. We must fight to win."

The older warriors shook their heads sorrowfully and spoke of younger days when they fought the Pawnees bravely, honorably, man-to-man. But I and several other young men wanted to learn how to control the Thunderbirds. And we knew Crazy Horse spoke the truth, that our lives would never be happy as long as there were white men in the world. Finally, because they could not forbid us to go with the Oglala, only advise against it and say that the Great Mystery had not intended us to fly, Red Horse and I and some others went with Crazy Horse. I did not see my village again, not even at the big camp on the Greasy Grass [Little Big Horn—MT] where we rubbed out Yellow Hair. I think perhaps the blueshirts came after I was gone and told Two Pines that he had to leave his home and come to this flat dead place.

The Oglala Crazy Horse taught us to fly the Thunderbirds. We learned a great many things about the Gray White Man's machines. With them, we killed Yellowleg flyers. Soon, I tired of the waiting and the hunger. We were raided once. It was a good fight. In the dark, we chased the Big Fish [the Indian word for dirigibles—MT] and killed many men on the ground.

I do not remember all of what happened those seasons. When we were finally chased away from the landing place, Crazy Horse had us hide the Thunderbirds in the Black Hills. I have heard the Yellowlegs did not know we had the Thun-

derbirds; that they thought they were run by the gray white
men only. It did not matter; we thought we had used them for
the last time.

Many seasons later, we heard what happened to Black Kettle's village. I went to the place sometime after the battle. I
heard that Crazy Horse had been there and seen the place. I
looked for him but he had gone north again. Black Kettle had
been a treaty man: we talked among ourselves that the
Yellowlegs had no honor.

It was the winter I was sick [1872. The Plains Indians and
the U. S. Army alike were plagued that winter by what we
would call the influenza. It was probably brought by some
itinerant French trapper.—MT] that I heard of Crazy Horse's
raid on the landing place of the Big Fish. It was news of this
that told us we must prepare to fight the Yellowlegs.

When I was well, my wives and I and Eagle Hawk's band
went looking for Crazy Horse. We found him in the fall. Already, the Army had killed many Sioux and Cheyenne that
summer. Crazy Horse said we must band together, we who
knew how to fly the Thunderbirds. He said we would someday
have to fight the Yellowlegs among the clouds as in the old
days. We only had five Thunderbirds which had not been
flown many seasons. We spent the summer planning to get
more. Red Chief and Yellow Dog gathered a large band. We
raided the Fort Kearny and stole many Thunderbirds and
canisters of powder. We hid them in the Black Hills. It had
been a good fight.

It was at this time Yellow Hair sent out many soldiers to
protect the miners he had brought in by speaking false. They
destroyed the sacred lands of the Sioux. We killed some of
them, and the Yellowlegs burned many of our villages. That
was not a good time. The Big Fish killed many of our people.

We wanted to get the Thunderbirds and kill the Big Fish.
Crazy Horse had us wait. He had been talking to Sitting Bull,
the Hunkpapa chief. Sitting Bull said we should not go
against the Yellowlegs yet, that we could only kill a few at a

time. Later, he said, they would all come. That would be the good day to die.

The next year, they came. We did not know until just before the Sun Dance [about June 10, 1876—MT] that they were coming. Crazy Horse and I and all those who flew the Thunderbirds went to get ours. It took us two days to get them going again, and we had only six Thunderbirds flying when we flew to stop the blueshirts. Crazy Horse, Yellow Dog, American Gun, Little Wolf, Big Tall, and I flew that day. It was a good fight. We killed two Big Fish and many men and horses. We stopped the Turtles-which-kill [that would be the light armored cars Crook had with him on the Rosebud River—MT] so they could not come toward the Greasy Grass where we camped. The Sioux under Spotted Pony killed more on the ground. We flew back and hid the Thunderbirds near camp.

When we returned, we told Sitting Bull of our victory. He said it was good, but that a bigger victory was to come. He said he had had a vision during the Sun Dance. He saw many soldiers and enemy Indians fall out of the sky on their heads into the village. He said ours was not the victory he had seen.

It was some days later we heard that a Yellowlegs Thunderbird had been shot down. We went to the place where it lay. There was a strange device above its wing. Crazy Horse studied it many moments. Then he said, "I have seen such a thing before. It carries Thunderbirds beneath one of the Big Fish. We must get our Thunderbirds. It will be a good day to die."

We hurried to our Thunderbirds. We had twelve of them fixed now, and we had on them, besides the quick rifles [Henry machine rifles of calibers .41-40 or .30-30—MT], the roaring spears [Hale spin-stabilized rockets, of 2½ inch diameter—MT]. We took off before noonday.

We arrived at the Greasy Grass and climbed into the clouds, where we scouted. Soon, to the south, we saw the dust of many men moving. But Crazy Horse held us back. Soon we saw why; four Big Fish were coming. We came at them out of the sun. They did not see us till we were on them. We fired our

roaring sticks, and the Big Fish caught fire and burned. All
except one, which drifted away, though it lost all its fat. Wild
Horse, in his Thunderbird, was shot but still fought on with us
that morning. We began to kill the men on the Big Fish when
a new thing happened. Men began to float down on blankets.
We began to kill them as they fell with our quick rifles. Then
we attacked those who reached the ground, until we saw Spotted Pony and his men were on them. We turned south and
killed many horse soldiers there. Then we flew back to the
Greasy Grass and hid the Thunderbirds. At camp, we learned
that many pony soldiers had been killed. Word came that
more soldiers were coming.

I saw, as the sun went down, the women moving among the
dead Men-Who-Float-Down, taking their clothes and supplies. They covered the ground like leaves in the autumn. It
had been a good fight.

"So much has been written about that hot June day in
1876, so much guesswork applied where knowledge was missing. Was Custer dead in his harness before he reached the
ground? Or did he stand and fire at the aircraft strafing his
men? How many reached the ground alive? Did any escape
the battle itself, only to be killed by Indian patrols later that
afternoon, or the next day? No one really knows, and all the
Indians are gone now, so history stands a blank.

"Only one thing is certain: for the men of the 7th Cavalry
there was only the reality of the exploding dirigibles, the snap
of their chutes deploying, the roar of the aircraft among them,
the bullets, and those terrible last moments on the bluff.
Whatever the verdict of their peers, whatever the future may
reveal, it can be said they did not die in vain."

—*The Seventh Cavalry: A History*
E. R. BURROUGHS
Colonel, U.S.A., Retired

SUGGESTED READING

ANONYMOUS. *Remember Ft. Sumter!* Washington: War Department Recruiting Pamphlet, 1862.

————. *Leviathans of the Skies.* Goodyear Publications, 1923.

————. *The Dirigible in War and Peace.* Goodyear Publications, 1911.

————. *Sitting Bull, Killer of Custer.* G. E. Putnam's, 1903.

————. *Comanche of the Seventh.* Chicago: Military Press, 1879.

————. *Thomas Edison and the Indian Wars.* Menlo Park, N.J.: Edison Press, 1921.

————. "Fearful Slaughter at Big Horn." New York: *Herald-Times,* July 8, 1876, *et passim.*

————. *Custer's Gold Hoax.* Boston: Barnum Press, 1892.

————. "Reno's Treachery: New Light on the Massacre at The Little Big Horn." Chicago: *Daily News-Mirror,* June 12–19, 1878.

————. "Grant Scandals and the Plains Indian Wars." *Life,* May 3, 1921.

————. *The Hunkpapa Chief Sitting Bull,* Famous Indians Series ⌗3. New York: 1937.

ARNOLD, HENRY H. *The Air War in the East,* Smithsonian Annals of Flight, Vol. 38. Four books, 1932–37.
1. *Sumter To Bull Run*
2. *Williamsburg to Second Manassas*
3. *Gettysburg to the Wilderness*
5. *The Bombing of Atlanta to Haldeman*

BALLOWS, EDWARD. *The Indian Ace: Crazy Horse.* G. E. Putnam's, 1903.

BENTEEN, CAPT. FREDERICK. *Major Benteen's Letters to his Wife.* University of Oklahoma Press, 1921.

BRININSTOOL, A. E. *A Paratrooper with Custer.* n.p.g., 1891.

BURROUGHS, COL. E. R. retired. *The Seventh Cavalry: A History.* Chicago: 1931.

CLAIR-BRITNER, EDOARD. *Haldeman: Where the War Ended.* Frankfort University Press, 1911.

CROOK, GENERAL GEORGE C. *Yellowhair: Custer as the Indians Knew Him.* Cincinnati Press, 1882.

CUSTER, GEORGE A. *My Life on the Plains and in the Clouds*. Chicago: 1874

———— and CUSTER, ELIZABETH. *'Chutes and Saddles*. Chicago: 1876.

Custer's Luck, n.a, n.p.g., [1891]

DE CAMP, L. SPRAGUE and PRATT, FLETCHER. *Franklin's Engine: Mover of the World*. Hanover House, 1939.

DE VOTO, BERNARD. *The Road From Sumter*. Scribners, 1931.

ELSEE, D. V. *The Last Raid of Crazy Horse*. Random House, 1921.

The 505th: History From the Skies. DA Pamphlet 870-10-3 GPO Pittsburgh, May 12, 1903.

FM 23-13-2 Machine Rifle M3121A1 and M3121A1E1 Cal. .41-40 Operator's Manual, DA FM, July 12, 1873.

GODDARD, ROBERT H. *Rocketry: From 400 B.C. to 1933*. Smithsonian Annals of Flight, Vol. 31, GPO Pittsburgh, 1934.

Guide to the Custer Battlefield National Monument. U. S. Parks Services, GPO Pittsburgh, 1937.

The Indian Wars. 3 vols, GPO Pittsburgh, 1898.

KALIN, DAVID. *Hook Up! The Story of the Balloon Infantry*. New York: 1932.

KELLOGG, MARK W. *The Drop at Washita*. Chicago: *Times Press,* 1872.

LOCKRIDGE, SGT. ROBERT. *History of the Airborne: From Shiloh to Ft. Bragg*. Chicago: Military Press, 1936.

LOWE, THADDEUS C. *Aircraft of the Civil War*. 4 vols. 1891–96.

MCCOY, COL. TIM. *The Vanished American*. Phoenix Press, 1934.

MCGOVERN, MAJ. WILLIAM. *Death in the Dakotas*. Sioux Press, 1889.

MORISON, SAMUEL ELIOT. *France in the New World 1627–1864*. 1931.

MYREN, GUNDAL. *The Sun Dance Ritual and the Last Indian Wars*. 1901.

PATTON, GEN. GEORGE C. *Custer's Last Campaigns*. Military House, 1937.

PAUL, WINSTON. *We Were There at the Bombing of Ft. Sumter*. Landmark Books, 1929.

PAYLEY, DAVID. *Where Custer Fell*. New York Press, 1931.

POWELL, MAJ. JOHN WESLEY. *Report on the Arid Lands*. GPO, 1881.

Proceedings, Reno Court of Inquiry. GPO Pittsburgh, 1881.

Report on the U.S.-Canadian Offensive against Sitting Bull, 1879. GPO Pittsburgh, War Department, 1880.

SANDBURG, CARL. *Mr. Lincoln's Airmen.* Chicago: Driftwind Press, 1921.

SETTLE, SGT. MAJ. WINSLOW. *Under the Crossed Sabers.* Military Press, 1898.

SHERIDAN, GEN. PHILLIP. *The Only Good Indian . . .* Military House, 1889.

SINGLETON, WILLIAM WARREN. *J. E. B. Stuart, Attila of the Skies.* Boston, 1871.

SMITH, GREGORY. *The Grey White Man: Moseby's Expedition to the Northwest 1863–1866.* University of Oklahoma Press, 1921.

SMITH, NELDOO. *He Gave Them Wings: Captain Smith's Journal 1861–1864.* Urbana: University of Illinois Press, 1927.

STEEN, NELSON. *Opening of the West.* Jim Bridger Press, 1902.

TAPSCOTT, RICHARD D. *He Came With the Comet.* University of Illinois Press, 1927.

TWAIN, MARK. *Huckleberry Among the Hostiles: A Journal.* Hutton Books, 1932.

*One of the great themes of science fiction is the desperate
weariness that would eventually wear down an immortal person:
the most resourceful and inventive of us could find enough
things to do for hundreds, thousands of years . . . but forever?
"Forever is too long," as one science fiction novel was titled a
quarter century ago.*

HARLAN ELLISON *tells now of a being who had lived far too
long, who has done everything there is to do, on a cosmic scale.
And of a Final Gathering of many such people, on a world of a
far star.*

The Wine Has Been
Left Open Too Long and
the Memory Has Gone Flat*

BY HARLAN ELLISON

*"Taking advantage of what he had heard with one limited pair
of ears, in a single and relatively isolated moment of recorded
history, in the course of an infinitesimal fraction of conceivable
time (which some say is the only time), he came to believe
firmly that there was much that he could not hear, much that
was constantly being spoken and indeed sung to teach him
things he could never otherwise grasp, which if grasped would
complete the fragmentary nature of his consciousness until it
was whole at last—one tone both pure and entire floating in
the silence of the egg, at the same pitch as the silence."*

W. S. MERWIN, "The Chart"[1]

Ennui was the reason only one hundred and one thousand alien representatives came to the Sonority Gathering. One hundred and one thousand out of six hundred and eleven thousand possible delegates, one each from the inhabited worlds of the stellar community. Even so, counterbalancing the poor turnout was the essential fact that it had been ennui, in the first place, that had caused the Gathering to be organized. Ennui, utter boredom, oppressive worlds-weariness, deep heaving sighs, abstracted vacant stares, familiar thoughts and familiar views.

The dance of entropy was nearing its end.

The orchestration of the universe sounded thick and gravelly, a tune slowing down inexorably, being played at the wrong speed.

Chasm ruts had been worn in the dance floor.

The oscillating universe was fifty billion years old, and it was tired.

And the intelligent races of six hundred and eleven thousand worlds sought mere moments of amusement, pale beads strung on a dreary Möbius of dragging time. Mere moments, each one dearer than the last, for there were so few. Everything that could be done, had been done; every effort was ultimately the fuzzed echo of an earlier attempt.

Even the Sonority Gathering had been foreshadowed by the Vulpeculan Quadrivium in '08, the tonal festival hosted by the Saturniidae of Whoung in '76, and the abortive, ludicrous Rigellian Sodality "musical get-together" that had turned out to be merely another fraudulent attempt to purvey the artist Merle's skiagrams to an already-disenchanted audience.

Nonetheless (in a phrase exhumed and popularized by the Recidivists of Fornax 993–λ), it was "the only game in town." And so, when the esteemed and shimmering DeilBo

---

1 From "The Chart" by W. S. Merwin, in *The New Yorker*, Oct. 22, 1973.

devised the Gathering, his reputation as an innovator and the crush of ennui combined to stir excitement of a sluggish sort . . . and one hundred and one thousand delegates came. To Vindemiatrix Σ in what had long ago been called, in the time of the heliocentric arrogance, the "constellation" of Virgo.

With the reddish-yellow eye of the giant Arcturus forever lighting the azure skies, forever vying with Spica's first magnitude brilliance, Σ's deserts and canyons seemed poor enough stage setting for the lesser glow of Vindemiatrix, forever taking third place in prominence to its brawny elders. But Σ, devoid of intelligent life, a patchwork-colored world arid and crumbling, had one thing to recommend it that DeilBo found compelling: the finest acoustics of any world in the universe.

The Maelstrom Labyrinth. Remnant of volcanic upheavals and the retreat of oceans and the slow dripping of acid waters, Σ boasted a grand canyon of stalagmites that rose one hundred and sixty kilometers; stalactites that narrowed into spear-tip pendants plunging down over ninety kilometers into bottomless crevasses; caverns and arroyos and tunnels that had never been plotted; the arching, golden stone walls had never been seen by the eyes of intelligent creatures; the Ephemeris called it the Maelstrom Labyrinth. No matter where one stood in the sixteen-hundred-kilometer sprawl of the Labyrinth, one could speak with a perfectly normal tone, never even raise one's voice, and be assured that a listener crouching deep in a cave at the farthest point of the formation could hear what he said as if beside him. DeilBo selected the Maelstrom Labyrinth as the site for the Gathering.

And so they came. One hundred and one thousand alien life-forms. From what the primitives had once called the constellations of Indus and Pavo, from Sad al Bari in Pegasus, from Mizar and Phecda, from all the worlds of the stellar community they came; bearing with them the special sounds they hoped would be judged the most extraordinary, the most stirring, the most memorable: ultimate sounds. They came, because they were bored and there was nowhere else to go;

they came, they wanted to hear what they had never heard before. They came; and they heard.

*". . . he domesticated the elephant, the cat, the bear, the rat,
and kept all the remaining whales in dark stalls, trying to hear
through their ears the note made by the rocking of the axle of
the earth."*

                                    W. S. MERWIN, "The Chart"

If she had one fear in this endless life, it was that she would be forced to be born again. Yes, of course, life was sacred, but how *long,* how ceaselessly, repetitiously long did it have to go on? Why were such terrible stigmas visited on the relatives and descendants of those who simply, merely, only wished to know the sweet sleep?

Stileen had tried to remember her exact age just a few solstices ago. Periodically she tried to remember; and only when she recognized that it was becoming obsessive did she put it out of her mind. She was very old, even by the standards of immortality of her race. And all she truly hungered to know, after all those times and stars, was the sweet sleep.

A sleep denied her by custom and taboo.

She sought to busy herself with diversions.

She had devised the system of gravity pulse-manipulation that had kept the dense, tiny worlds of the Neer 322 system from falling into their Primary. She had compiled the exhaustive concordance of extinct emotions of all the dead races that had ever existed in the stellar community. She had assumed control of the Red Line Armies in the perpetual Procyon War for over one hundred solstices, and had amassed more confirmed tallies than any other commander-in-chief in the War's long history.

Her insatiable curiosity and her race's longevity had combined to provide the necessary state of mind that would lead her, inevitably, to the sound. And having found it, and having perceived what it was, and being profoundly ready to enjoy the sweet sleep, she had come to the Gathering to share it with the rest of the stellar community.

For the first time in millennia, Stileen was not seeking merely to amuse herself; she was engaged on a mission of significance . . . and finality.

With her sound, she came to the Gathering.

She was ancient, deep yellow, in her jar with cornsilk hair floating free in the azure solution. DeilBo's butlers took her to her assigned place in the Labyrinth, set her down on a limestone ledge in a deep cavern where the acoustics were particularly rich and true, tended to her modest needs, and left her.

Stileen had time, then, to dwell on the diminished enthusiasm she had for continued life.

DeilBo made the opening remarks, heard precisely and clearly throughout the Maelstrom. He used no known language, in fact used no words. Sounds, mere sounds that keynoted the Gathering by imparting his feelings of warmth and camaraderie to the delgates. In every trench and run and wash and cavern of the Maelstrom, the delegates heard, and in their special ways smiled with pleasure, even those without mouths or the ability to smile.

It was to be, truly, a Sonority Gathering, in which sounds alone would be judged. Impressed, the delegates murmured their pleasure.

Then DeilBo offered to present the first sound for their consideration. He took the responsibility of placing himself first, as a gesture of friendship, an icebreaker of a move. Again, the delegates were pleased at the show of hospitality, and urged DeilBo to exhibit his special sound.

And this is the sound, the ultimate sound, the very special sound he had trapped for them:

On the eleventh moon of the world called Chill by its inhabitants, there is a flower whose roots are sunk deep, deep into the water pools that lie far beneath the black stone sur-

face. This flower, without a name, seems to be an intricate construct of spiderwebs. There are, of course, no spiders on the eleventh moon of Chill.

Periodically, for no reason anyone has ever been able to discern, the spiderweb flowers burst into flame, and very slowly destroy themselves, charring and shriveling and turning to ashes that lie where they fall. There is no wind on the eleventh moon of Chill.

During the death ceremonies of the spiderweb flowers, the plants give off a haunting and terrible sound. It is a song of colors. Shades and hues that have no counterparts anywhere in the stellar community.

DeilBo had sent scavengers across the entire face of Chill's eleventh moon, and they had gathered one hundred of the finest spiderweb flowers, giants among their kind. DeilBo had talked to the flowers for some very long time prior to the Gathering. He had told them what they had been brought to the Maelstrom to do, and though they could not speak, it became apparent from the way they straightened in their vats of enriched water (for they had hung their tops dejectedly when removed from the eleventh moon of Chill) that they took Deil-Bo's purpose as a worthy fulfillment of their destiny, and would be proud to burn on command.

So DeilBo gave the gentle command, speaking sounds of gratitude and affection to the spiderweb flowers, who burst into flame and sang their dangerous song of death. . . .

It began with blue, a very ordinary blue, identifiable to every delegate who heard it. But the blue was only the ground coat; in an instant it was overlaid with skirls of a color like wind through dry stalks of harvested grain. Then a sea color the deepest shade of a blind fish tooling through algae-thick waters. Then the color of hopelessness collided with the color of desperation and formed a nova of hysteria that in the human delegates sounded exactly like the color of a widower destroying himself out of loneliness.

The song of colors went on for what seemed a long time,

though it was only a matter of minutes, and when it faded away into ashes and was stilled, they all sat humbled and silent, wishing they had not heard it.

Stileen revolved slowly in her jar, troubled beyond consolation at the first sound the Gathering had proffered. For the first time in many reborn lifetimes, she felt pain. A sliver of glass driven into her memories. Bringing back the clear, loud sound of a moment when she had rejected one who had loved her. She had driven him to hurt her, and then he had sunk into a deathly melancholy, a silence so deep no words she could summon would serve to bring him back. And when he had gone, she had asked for sleep, and they had given it to her . . . only to bring her life once again, all too soon.

In her jar, she wept.

And she longed for the time when she could let them hear the sound she had found, the sound that would release her at last from the coil of mortality she now realized she despised with all her soul.

After a time, the first delegate—having recovered from DeilBo's offering—ventured forth with its sound. It was an insect creature from a world named Joumell, and this was the sound it had brought:

Far beneath a milky sea on a water world of Joumell's system, there is a vast grotto whose walls are studded with multicolored quartz crystals whose cytoplasmic cell contents duplicate the filament curves of the galaxies NGC 4038 and NGC 4039. When these crystals mate, there is a perceptible encounter that produces tidal tails. The sounds of ecstasy these crystals make when they mate is one long, sustained sigh of rapture that is capped by yet another, slightly higher and separate from the preceding. Then another, and another, until a symphony of crystalline orgasms is produced no animal throats could match.

The insect Joumelli had brought eleven such crystals (the

minimum number required for a sexual coupling) from the
water world. A cistern formation had been filled with a white
crystalline acid, very much like cuminoin; it initiated a cyto-
taxian movement; a sexual stimulation. The crystals had been
put down in the cistern and now they began their mating.

The sound began with a single note, then another joined and
overlay it, then another, and another. The symphony began
and modulations rose on modulations, and the delegates closed
their eyes—even those who had no eyes—and they basked in
the sound, translating it into the sounds of joy of their various
species.

And when it was ended, many of the delegates found the
affirmation of life permitted them to support the memory of
DeilBo's terrible death melody of the flowers.

Many did not.

> ". . . the frequencies of their limits of hearing . . . a calendar
> going forward and backward but not in time, even though time
> was the measure of the frequencies as it was the measure of
> every other thing (therefore, some say, the only measure) . . ."
>   W. S. MERWIN, "The Chart"

She remembered the way they had been when they had first
joined energies. It had been like that sound, the wonderful
sound of those marvelous crystals.

Stileen turned her azure solution opaque, and let herself
drift back on a tide of memory. But the tide retreated, leaving
her at the shore of remembrance where DeilBo's sound still
lingered, dark and terrible. She knew that even the trembling
threads of joy unforgotten could not sustain her, and she
wanted to let them hear what she had brought. There was
simply too much pain in the universe, and if she—peculiarly
adapted to contain such vast amounts of anguish—could not
live with it . . . there must be an end. It was only humane.

She sent out a request to be put on the agenda as soon as
possible and DeilBo's butlers advised her she had a time to

wait; and as her contact was withdrawn, she brushed past a creature reaching out for a position just after hers. When she touched its mind, it closed off with shocking suddenness. Afraid she had been discourteous, Stileen went away from the creature quickly, and did not reach out again. But in the instant she had touched it, she had glimpsed something . . . it would not hold. . . .

The sounds continued, each delegate presenting a wonder to match the wonders that had gone before.

The delegate from RR Lyrae IV produced the sound of a dream decaying in the mind of a mouselike creature from Bregga, a creature whose dreams formed its only reality. The delegate from RZ Cephei Beta VI followed with the sound of ghosts in the Mountains of the Hand; they spoke of the future and lamented their ability to see what was to come. The delegate from Ennore came next with the sound of red, magnified till it filled the entire universe. The delegate from Gateway offered the sound of amphibious creatures at the moment of their mutation to fully land-living vertebrates; there was a wail of loss at that moment, as their chromosomes begged for return to the warm, salty sea. The delegates from Algol C XXIII gave them the sounds of war, collected from every race in the stellar community, broken down into their component parts, distilled, purified, and recast as one tone; it was numbing. The delegate from Blad presented a triptych of sound: a sun being born, the same sun coasting through its main stage of hydrogen burning, the sun going nova—a shriek of pain that phased in and out of normal space-time with lunatic vibrations. The delegate from Iobbaggii played a long and ultimately boring sound that was finally identified as a neutrino passing through the universe; when one of the other delegates suggested that sound, being a vibration in a medium, could not be produced by a neutrino passing through vacuum, the Iobbaggiian responded—with pique—that the sound produced had been the sound *within* the neutrino; the querying delegate then said it must have taken a *very* tiny microphone to pick up the sound; the Iobbaggiian stalked out of the Gathering on his eleven-meter stilts. When the uproar died away, the agenda was moved and the delegate from Kruger 60B IX delivered up a potpourri of sounds of victory and satisfaction and joy and innocence and pleasure from a gathering of microscopic species inhabiting a grain of sand in the Big Desert region of Catrimani; it was a patchwork quilt of delights that helped knit together the Gathering. Then the delegate from the Opal Cluster (his specific world's native name was taboo and could not be used) assaulted them with a sound none could identify, and when it had faded away into trembling silence, leaving behind only the memory of cacophony, he told the Gathering that it was the sound of chaos; no one doubted his word. The delegate from Mainworld followed with the sound of a celestial choir composed of gases being blown away from a blue star in a rosette nebula ten light-years across; all the angels of antiquity could not have sounded more glorious.

And then it was Stileen's turn, and she readied the sound that would put an end to the Gathering.

"And beyond—and in fact among—the last known animals living and extinct, the lines could be drawn through white spaces that had an increasing progression of their own, into regions of hearing that was no longer conceivable, indicating creatures wholly sacrificed or never evolved, hearers of the note at which everything explodes into light, and of the continuum that is the standing still of darkness, drums echoing the last shadow without relinquishing the note of the first light, hearkeners to the unborn overflowing."

W. S. MERWIN, "The Chart"

"There is no pleasure in this," Stileen communicated, by thought and by inflection. "But it is the sound that I have found, the sound I know you would want me to give to you

. . . and you must do with it what you must. I am sorry."

And she played for them the sound.

It was the sound of the death of the universe. The dying gasp of their worlds and their suns and their galaxies and their island universes. The death of all. The final sound.

And when the sound was gone, no one spoke for a long time, and Stileen was at once sad, but content: now the sleep would come, and she would be allowed to rest.

"The delegate is wrong."

The silence hung shrouding the moment. The one who had spoken was a darksmith from Luxann, chief world of the Logomachy. Theologians, pragmatists, reasoners *sans appel,* his words fell with the weight of certainty.

"It is an oscillating universe," he said, his cowl shrouding his face, the words emerging from darkness. "It will die, and it will be reborn. It has happened before, it will happen again."

And the tone of the Gathering grew brighter, even as Stileen's mood spiraled down into despair. She was ambivalent—pleased for them, that they could see an end to their ennui and yet perceive the rebirth of life in the universe—desolate for herself, knowing somehow, some way, she would be recalled from the dead.

And then the creature she had passed in reaching out for her place on the agenda, the creature that had blocked itself to her mental touch, came forward in their minds and said, "There is another sound beyond hers."

This was the sound the creature let them hear, the sound that had *always* been there, that had existed for time beyond time, that could not be heard though the tone was always with them; and it could be heard now only because it existed as it passed through the instrument the creature made of itself.

It was the sound of reality, and it sang of the end *beyond* the end, the final and total end that said without possibility of argument, *There will be no rebirth because we have never existed.*

Whatever they had thought they were, whatever arrogance

had brought their dream into being, it was now coming to final moments, and beyond those moments there was nothing.

No space, no time, no life, no thought, no gods, no resurrection and rebirth.

The creature let the tone die away, and these who could reach out with their minds to see what it was, were turned back easily. It would not let itself be seen.

The messenger of eternity had only anonymity to redeem itself . . . for whom?

And for Stileen, who did not even try to penetrate the barriers, there was no pleasure in the knowledge that it had all been a dream. For if it had been a dream, then the joy had been a dream as well.

It was not easy to go down to emptiness, never having tasted joy. But there was no appeal.

In the Maelstrom Labyrinth, there was no longer ennui.

*So many people talk about our energy crisis, so many
suggestions are made, from installing offshore windmills to
tapping the thermal heat produced by animal droppings . . .
yet no one (until John Shirley) has suggested that we use the
most reliable form of energy in the universe: entropy. Here he
tells of a future world in which death-energy has at last been
harnessed for living. Of course, there are complications. . . .*

JOHN SHIRLEY *is a graduate of the Clarion SF Writers'
Workshops and has sold stories to* Clarion, New Dimensions,
*and others. He writes with an original voice, and you'll be seeing
much more from him.*

Under the Generator

BY JOHN SHIRLEY

Looking into the eyes of the woman who sat across from him
in the crowded cafeteria, he was reminded of the eyes of another woman entirely. Perhaps there were secret mirrors hidden in the faces of the two women. He remembered the other
woman, Alice, when she had said: *I just can't continue with
you if you insist on keeping that damn job. I'm sorry, Ronnie,
but I just can't. My personal convictions leave no room for
those inhuman generators.*

He reflected, looking into the eyes of the second woman,
that he could have quit the job for Alice. But he hadn't.
Maybe he hadn't actually wanted her. And he had gone easily
from Alice to Donna. He resolved not to lose Donna too because of his work with the generators.

"I used to be an actor," Denton said. Swirling coffee in his
cup, he shifted uncomfortably in the cafeteria seat and wondered if the plastic of the cup would melt slightly into the
coffee. . . . Working at the hospital, drinking coffee every

morning and noon out of the same white-mold sort of cups, he
had visions of the plastic slowly coating the interior of his
stomach with white brittle.

"What happened to acting and how far'd you get?" Donna
Farber asked with her characteristic way of cramming as
much inquiry as she could into one line.

Denton frowned, his wide mouth making an elaborate
squiggle across his broad, pale face. His expressions were always slightly exaggerated, as if he were an actor not yet used
to the part of Ronald Denton.

"I was working off-Broadway, and I had a good part in a
play I wrote myself. An actor can always play the part better
if he wrote it. The play was called *All Men Are Created
Sequels*. Tigner produced it."

"Never heard of it."

"Naturally it fell flat after I pulled out."

"Naturally." Her silver-flecked blue eyes laughed.

"Anyway, I felt that acting was stealing too much of my
identity. Or something. Actually, I'm not sure just why I quit.
Maybe it was really stage fright."

His unexpected candor brought her eyes to his. He remembered Alice and wondered how to discover just how Donna
felt about his job, if she felt anything at all.

But the subject was primed by his black uniform. "Why did
you quit acting to work in the generators?"

"I don't know. It was available and it had good hours. Four
hours a day, four days a week, twelve dollars an hour."

"Yeah . . . but it must be depressing to work there. I mean,
you probably still haven't been able to give up acting entirely.
You have to act like there's nothing wrong around people
who are going to die soon." There was no indictment in her
tone. Her head tilted sympathetically.

Denton just nodded as if he had found sorrowful virtue in
being the scapegoat. "Somebody has to do it," he said. Actually, he was elated. He had been trying to arouse interest from
Donna for a week. He looked at her frankly, admiring her
slender hands wrapped around her coffeecup, the soft cone of

her lips blowing to cool the coffee, close flaxen hair cut into a bowl behind her ears.

"I don't entirely understand," she said, looking for a divination in her coffee, "why they didn't get the retired nurses or someone used to death for the job."

"For one thing, you need a little electronic background to keep watch on the generators. That's what got me the job. I studied electronics before I was an actor."

"That's a strange contrast. Electronics and acting."

"Not really. Both involve knowledge of circuitry. But anyway, not even experienced nurses are used to sitting there *watching* people die for four hours at a time. They usually let them alone except when administering—"

"But I thought you said all you had to do was sit and check the dials every so often. You mean you have to watch?"

"Well . . . you can't help it. You sit right across from the patient. Since you're there, you look. I'm aware of them, anyhow, because I have to make sure they aren't dying too fast for the machine to scoop."

She was silent, looking around the busy lunchroom as if seeking support from the milling, wooden-faced hospital employees. She seemed to be listening for a tempo in the clashing of dishes and the trapped rumble of conversations.

Denton was afraid that he had offended her, giving her the impression that he was a vulture. He hoped that she wasn't looking around for someone else to talk to. . . .

"I don't like it in here," she said, her voice a small life to itself. "I think it's because in most kitchens you hear the clinking noises of china and glass. Here it's scraping plastic." One side of her mouth pulled into an ironic smile.

"Let's go outside then," Denton said, a trifle too eagerly.

They discarded their trays in the recycling chute and walked to the elevator. Denton was silent as they rode to the ground floor of the huge hospital; he didn't want to converse, irrationally afraid that the giddy elevator box might trap their words in the sliding doors, to carry them off to strangers.

They emerged into the pastel curves of the hospital lobby,

walking between artificial potted palms and people waiting with artificial expressions concealing worry. They went out the sussurating front doors, from the odor of disinfectant into June sunlight and the warm breathing of air-cars.

"I'm glad all the engines are turbines now," she remarked. "They're so quiet. No tires on the street squealing and no growling pistons and just air to wash my face in. All the noise of traffic used to scare me when I was little." They talked quietly of cars and the city and their jobs until they came to the park.

Sitting under a tree, plucking absently at the grass, they were silent for a while, feeling the ambience of the bustling park.

Until without provocation Donna began: "My parents died five years ago and—" Then she stopped and looked at him sideways. She shook her head.

"Were you going to say something else?"

She shook her head again, too quickly. He wanted to ask if they had put generators over her parents before they'd died; but he decided that the question might put him in a bad light.

They sat in the park and watched bicyclers and children sift through the plasphalt paths. After a while a slush vendor rolled a sticky white cart past, and Denton got up to buy two drinks. He was just returning from the vendor, about thirty feet from where Donna waited under the tree, when someone put a hand on his right arm.

"Can I talk to you?" A subdued tone. "Just for a minute?" It was a boy, perhaps sixteen, but at least three inches taller than Denton. The boy kept opening and closing his mouth pensively, questions anxious to spring from his lips. He was dressed in a denim body suit. His hands were thrust deep into his side-pockets, as if leashed. Denton nodded, glancing at the slushes to make certain that they wouldn't melt on his hands. Probably the kid was proselytizing for one of the burgeoning Satanic cults.

"You're a generator guy, aren't you? A compensator."

Denton nodded dumbly again.

"My father's under a generator; he's dying. And he ain't old or useless yet. He's still . . . needed." He paused to steady himself. "Can you . . . Maybe you could help him, turn off the machine for a while?" It was obvious that the boy wasn't used to asking favors. He resented having to ask Denton for anything.

Denton wished that he hadn't worn his uniform out of the hospital.

"I can't do anything for your father. I'm not a doctor. And there are dozens of generators in use at the hospital now. I've probably never seen your old man. Anyway, it isn't true that the generators steal strength from patients. It's an old wive's tale. It wouldn't do your father one bit of good if I turned it off. Sorry—" He began to walk toward Donna.

"What's your name?" the boy asked from behind, all respect gone from his tone. Denton could feel the boy's eyes on his back. He turned half around, miffed.

"Denton," he replied, immediately wishing that he had given a false name. He turned his back on the boy and walked back to Donna. He could feel an icy trail of slush melting over his hand.

"What did that kid want?" Donna asked, sipping her slush.

"Nothing. Directions to . . . the auditorium. He said he was going to the Satanist/Jeezus Freak confrontation."

"Really? He didn't look to be armed." She shrugged.

The boy was watching them.

Some of the slush had spilled onto Denton's leg. Donna wiped at the red stain on his black uniform with a white handkerchief.

He didn't want to think of work now. He had a date to take her to the Media Stew tonight. Finally: the first relationship he'd attempted since Alice.

But Denton decided it might be better to keep his mind on work. If he thought about her too much he would be nervous and contrived when he was with her. Maybe blow it. He tightened the belt around his one-piece jet uniform and went

quietly into the arbiter's office. The arbiter of compensators
was short, Jewish, and a compulsive caviler. Mr. Buxton
smiled as Denton bent over the worksheet titled WEEK OF
JUNE 19 THROUGH 26, 1986.

"What's your hurry, Denton? You young cats are always in
a hurry. You'll be assigned soon enough. You might find it
too soon. I haven't written you into the chart yet."

"Leave me on Mr. Hurzbau's generator, sir, if you would. I
get along well with Hurzbau."

"What is this "get along' junk? We bend the rule a little
that says no fraternizing with the patients under generators
. . . but *familiarity* is strictly verboten. You'll go nuts if
you—"

Not wanting to become embroiled in another of Buxton's
lectures, Denton quickly capitulated. "I'm sorry, sir. I didn't
mean to imply we knew each other well. What I meant was,
Hurzbau doesn't worry me much, or talk to me past the usual
amenities. Could I have my assignment now? I don't want the
unwatched generator to overload."

"Somebody's watching the generator all the time, naturally.
It can't over—"

"That's what I mean," Denton interrupted impatiently.
"The guy who's watching it is going to overload if he has to
work past his shift. He'll blame me."

"You should cultivate patience. Especially with your job."
Buxton shrugged his wide shoulders and put a thick hand on
his paunch. He regarded the chart, yawned, scratched his
bushy black mustache, and began to fill his pipe.

Denton, still standing, shifted uncomfortably. He wanted to
get his shift over with.

Buxton lit his pipe and blew gray smoke at Denton.

"Durghemmer today," Buxton said.

Denton frowned, dismayed. Durghemmer the leech.

"Durghemmer . . ." Denton spoke the name into the air so
that it would permanently leave his lips. "No. No, really, Buxton, I—"

"Just as I thought. Another weakling. I can never find anybody willing to take care of Durghemmer's generator, but I'll be damned if I'll end up doing it myself. So, Denton—"

"I can't. Really. I have a date tonight. Very delicate Psychological Balance involved. Durghemmer would ruin me." Denton looked with all his actor's pathos into his supervisor's eyes. Buxton stared at his hands, then relit his pipe.

"Okay. This time I let you off," he said. "Take Hurzbau. But don't talk to him unless it's absolutely necessary. I'm not supposed to, but I'll put Durghemmer's generator on automatic for tonight. It's dangerous but what the hell. But— Everybody's got to circulate sooner or later, Ron."

"Sure," said Denton, relieved. "Later." He took his punchcard from the rack on Buxton's office wall.

Denton read the dials punctiliously, reminding himself that this particular generator provided power for at least three hundred people. Amplitude was climbing. Poor Hurzbau. But thoughts like those, he told himself, were precisely the sort he didn't want. Good luck to Hurzbau.

Denton adjusted the position of the scoop over the bed. The scoop of the generator was a transparent bell enclosing the bed upon which Hurzbau rested. It was made of nonconductive fiberglass, veined with copper and platinum wiring which converged in a cable at its peak and twined like a thick metal vine through branches of metal supports into an opening in the cylindrical crystal in the generator's flat top.

The bulk of the rectangular generator transformer was opened in a honeycomb of metallic hexagons of the side facing the bed. On the other side Denton sat in his swivel chair, in his black uniform, in his controlled aplomb, behind his desk of dials and meters. Denton was officially the *compensator*, adjusting the rise and fall of energy absorbed by the generator so that a steady, predictable flow went out to the electrical transmitters.

Having checked the meters, Denton tried to relax for a while. He looked abstractedly around the room. The chamber was small, all white, with only the few paintings which Hurz-

bau's relatives had hung to cheer him up. The paintings were
of pastoral scenes from places mostly now entombed in
plasphalt.

Denton wondered why anyone had bothered with the paintings. Hurzbau couldn't see them except as vague blurs
through the plastic scoop. Nothing extraneous to the function
of the generator was allowed under the scoop. Not even bedclothes. Hurzbau's naked, cancer-eaten body was kept warm
with heaters.

Half of Hurzbau's face was eaten away by cancer. He had
once been overweight. He had gone from 220 pounds to 130
in four months. The right half of his face was sunken in to a
thin mask of skin clinging to the skull, and his right eye was
gone, the socket stuffed with cotton. He could talk only with
difficulty. His right arm was withered and unusable, though
his left was strong enough to prop him up on his elbow, allow-
ing him to seek Denton's attention.

"Compensator . . ." he rasped, barely audible through the
plastic. Denton switched on the intercom.

"What can I do for you, sir?" he asked, a trifle brusquely.
"Would you like me to call the nurse? I am not privileged to
give out medical aid personally. . . ."

"No. No nurse. Denton? That your name?"

"Yes. Ronald Denton. I told you yesterday, I believe. How
are—" He'd almost forgotten, but he caught himself in time.
He *knew* how Hurzbau was . . . the invalid was in constant
pain with six weeks to live, optimum. "Do you want to take
some metrazine? That I can get."

"No. You know what, Denton?" His voice was a raven's
croak.

"Look, I've been told I'm overfraternizing with the patients.
That's not really my job. We have a capable staff psychiatrist
and a priest and—"

"Who says you're not a priest, Denton? The other compensators don't talk to me at all. You're the only one who says a
damn thing to me. . . ." Hurzbau swallowed, his dessicated
features momentarily contorting so that the left half of his

face matched the malformation of the right. "You know, Denton, I could have gotten the cancer vaccine but I thought I'd never have need for it. Not *me*." He made some sandpapery noises which might have been akin to laughter. "And it's a sure thing if you get the cancer vaccine you *can't* get cancer, and I turned down a sure thing. Too much bother."

Denton suddenly felt cold toward the dying man. He recoiled inwardly, as if Hurzbau were a deformed siren trying to lure him under the scoop. It was true in a way: Hurzbau wanted sympathy. And sympathy would mean that Denton would have to imagine himself in Hurzbau's place. He shuddered. He had worked at the generator for six months but never before had a patient confided in him. He had to cut it off, even if it was at Hurzbau's expense.

But he was deterred by a look in the old man's eyes: a red light from the burning, blackened wick of Hurzbau's nerve-endings.

"Denton, tell me something. . . ." An almost visible wave of pain swept over Hurzbau's shrunken body; the parchment-thin skin of his face twisted as if it were about to rip. "Denton, I want to know. The generators, do they make me weaker? I know they . . . take energy . . . from my dying. . . . Do they . . . feed off me? Do they make me die so that—"

"No!" Denton was surprised at the stridency of his own exclamation. "No, you've got it turned around. It takes energies emitted because of your dying, but it doesn't come directly from *you*."

"Could you—" Hurzbau began, but he fell back on the bed, unable to keep himself propped up any longer. Drawn by inexplicable impulse, Denton got out of the control seat and walked around to the end of the bed. He looked down into the fading man's eyes, judging the advance of histolysis by the growth of an almost visible smoldering glow of pain. Hurzbau's mouth worked silently, furiously. Finally, tugging at the intravenous feeding tube imbedded in his left arm, he managed: "Denton . . . could you fix the generator if it broke down?"

"No. I don't know how it works. I just compensate for metrical oscillation—"

"Uh-huh. Then can you really say that it doesn't take away from my life if you don't know for sure how it works? You know what they *tell* you. But how do you know it's the truth?"

Hurzbau began to choke, spitting up yellow fluid. A moisture detector at the bedside prompted a plastic arm to stretch from the table of automatic instruments ensconced left of Hurzbau's head. The arm swabbed the pillow and Hurzbau's lips with a sponge. The light flared faintly in the dying man's eyes and with his good arm he swiped angrily at the mechanical swab.

"Damn, damn," he muttered, "I'm not a pool ball." The plastic strut fled back to its clamp.

Denton turned away, deliberately breaking the minor rapport developing between the two of them. But doubts insinuated through his stiffly starched black uniform. Maybe Hurzbau had been a criminal whom they'd deliberately infected as an energy reserve— But no, Durghemmer had been a respected politician, never convicted of anything; so how could one explain *his* interment under the generator? The man under the generator on the floor below had been a policeman. *No.* The principle behind the generators was taught in high school, and there were classes on the inner construction of the machines in vocational schools. There would be no way for the arbiters to hide anything from anyone. . . . There was no secret. But he understood Hurzbau's apprehensions. Even from his vantage point, perpetually on the bed, Hurzbau could see the two red dials side by side like mocking eyes, their needles climbing visibly whenever he got weaker.

He got weaker, the machine got stronger.

"Maybe it's something they're keeping under wraps, Denton," Hurzbau ventured suddenly. He spasmed then, rising almost to a sitting position, every muscle strained so that his skin was elasticized vitreously taut, making his withered frame mottle red. From between gritted teeth came Hurzbau's whisper, slightly metallic through the intercom: "How is there *room* for this much pain in this little body? There's enough to fill a warehouse. How does it all fit?" Denton turned off the intercom.

He rang for the nurse. The old man fell back, relaxing. Without wanting to, Denton glanced at the needle on the generator facing. It was climbing. He could hear the scoop humming. He ran around to the control panel and dialed to compensate for the upsurge in entropic energy. When the machine took in a great deal of energy at one time, it reacted with a high-frequency oscillating tone, very much like shrill laughter.

The generator chuckled, the old man grew weaker, the needles jumped higher. Hurzbau's body began to jerk and with each erratic rictus Denton's stomach contracted with revulsion. He had thought he was used to the onset of death.

Denton tightened the arm draped casually about Donna's creamy shoulders. She was asleep, or pretended to be. His casual posture lied about his inner turmoil. Inside, he seethed, remembering Donna's long boyish body like a graceful jet of water, thrashing with his. She'd responded only to the lightest touches. The visions of Donna alternated with memories of Hurzbau which Denton strove to suppress. But Hurzbau had thrashed in agony as she had writhed in ecstasy. Denton sat abruptly up to light a cigarette, throwing a tobacco smokescreen between himself and the recollection of the dying man.

He glanced down at Donna, saw her looking at him out of slitted eyes. She smiled hastily and looked away.

"What time is it?" she asked, her voice weary.

"One-A.M."

"What was your play about, anyway?"

"Do you want to read it? I have a copy—"

"No." Then she added, "I'm *interested,* but I don't like to read much these days. I had to read immensely before my internship. Medical textbooks ruined my appetite. I like live plays better. Why don't you perform it for me?"

He raised a hand melodramatically over her head and with an exaggeratedly visionary look that made her laugh, he quoth:

" 'We have come to bury Caesar, not to praise him . . .' "

"Oh, I see. That's from your play? You wrote that, eh?"

"Well, it's one I wrote a few centuries ago—"

"SHUT UP IN THERE I GOTTA GET SOME SLEEP! YOU ALREADY MADE ENOUGH NOISE GRUNTIN' TO KEEP THE WHOLE BUILDING AWAKE TILL DECEMBER!" a male voice shouted from the next apartment.

"The walls are thin," Denton whispered apologetically. But Donna was crying. She was sitting up, taller than Denton by half a head, rocking back and forth. He put an arm on her leg but she pushed away and got out of bed, throwing the bedclothes askew.

"Listen," Denton said frantically, "I'm sorry about that creep next door. Let's go somewhere—"

"No, it's okay. I'm going home. I had a good time and all that, you're a good lover, only . . ."

"Only *what?*"

She had her suit on already, she was putting on her shoes. He wondered what he had done. Better stop her before she gets dressed or she'll feel obligated to leave once she's gone that far. She was putting on her coat.

"What is it?" he asked with growing anxiety. "What did I do wrong?"

"Nothing. I just don't know why I came here, really. I don't need anyone to tell me I'm human. It's not good to get attached, anyway." She was heading toward the door as she spoke.

"SHUT UP IN THERE ALREADY!" the man next door shouted.

"GO TO HELL!" Denton shouted back. He pulled on one of his uniforms. She went out the door, leaving him alone with all the noises of the city night, rumbling through the open window like a hungry belly. "Damn!" Denton said aloud, fumbling at buttons.

Suddenly, apartments on three sides erupted, combining to grind the quiet evening into fine dust.

"ALL OF YOU CUT IT OUT!"

"I'LL BURN THIS HOLE TO THE GROUND IF YOU—"

"I'M GONNA CALL THE PIGS!"

Donna was stepping primly into the elevator just as Denton closed the door to his apartment behind him. He ran to the stairs and jogged swiftly down three flights, his footsteps echoing in the deserted concrete stairwell like the laughter of the generator.

He ran into the empty street. The night was muggy, warm with summer smugness. He spotted Donna halfway down the block to his left. He ran after her, feeling foolish, but shouting "Hey, wait! It's not that easy!"

She passed a black alleyway, turned the corner. He scuffled across the mouth of the alley, saw her disappear around the corner—

—something kicked his legs out from under him. He threw up his arms, felt the concrete edge of the curb crack an elbow, romancandling his arm; cheek striking the gutter grate: pain with snapping wires, cracking bullwhips. A hand pulled him roughly onto his back and he was looking at the twisted face of a teenage boy, ugly from barely repressed hatred. Someone else behind jerked Denton to his feet. His right eye was swelling and it hurt to squint, but with the other eye he saw that there were four hoods in all, each wearing transparent plastic jackets under which they were nude, muscular, and bristling with dark hairs. In sharp contrast to their hirsute lower parts, their faces and heads were shaved absolutely hairless. Their eyes burned with amphetamines. The drug made their maneuverings slightly spastic, like children flinching from expected blows.

Two of them held Denton's arms from behind. A third stepped in close with a knife. All four were strangely silent, almost pious. Denton saw the knife gleaming near his throat. He was paralyzed, numbed by what *should* have been unreality. He was watching viddy, he thought desperately. A commercial would come on in a moment. But one of the boys pulled Denton's head back by his hair with a violent twist that sent spotlights of pain into the growing darkness in his skull. The darkness congealed into abject fear. He was without volition. He remembered Donna. He looked around desperately without moving his head. Had she deliberately brought him here to meet these men? Had she set him up? What would they do with the knife?

One of the boys flicked quick fingers to unbutton Denton's shirt. He parted the folds of the black uniform slowly, almost formally, as if he were undressing a lover. Denton knew the night was warm but he felt the air in his open shirt cold as a knife blade. If he shouted for help they would probably kill him right away. The streetlight overhead hurt his eyes; his arms were cramping uncomfortably behind him. He tried to change position and was rewarded with a kneejab in the small of his back. He looked around for Donna as the knife cut open his undershirt (a very sharp knife, he noted; the fabric parted easily, as if it had been unzipped). Then he felt the knife on his navel, pain like a tiny point of intense light flaring up, and a trickle of warm blood. Already the warmth of shock enveloped him in surrender. He closed his eyes and bit his lips against the sting near his navel. The pain made him open them again.

The boy with the knife closed his eyes as if in anticipation of sybaritic satisfaction.

A blur of movement—

Then the boy with the knife screamed, his head snapped back, his mouth gaping, his back arched; he went rigid, yelling, "Damn! Who—"

He fell and Donna jumped easily aside and turned to face another. Denton felt the grip at the back of his neck relax as the boy behind him ran to aid his companion lying on the ground in front of her. Donna shot her booted foot, heel first, straight up and out, catching the third tough in the throat. She was tall and her long legs held her in good stead as the other two tried to get in close with their knives. The first two were lying almost like lovers on the ground; the boy who'd threatened Denton with the knife lay with his eyes wide open, unblinking, staring upward. He was perfectly still. The other was on his hands and knees, coughing blood onto his supine companion, one hand on his own crushed windpipe, his face staring and fascinated, as if he were tasting real pain for the first time, exploring it as a new world.

Stopping another with a shoe-point in the groin, Donna spun and, without wasting momentum, came forward onto the foot and transferred the motion to her arm, striking the knife from his hand. The knife rang on the concrete, rolling in front of the boy with the crushed throat.

Denton was breathing in huge gulps, still unable to act: he was sure that he would only run up against a television screen if he tried to intervene. But without a weapon, the last standing tough turned and fled into an alley.

The other boy was still clutching his groin, rocking back and forth on his haunches, moaning, his face draining. Donna regarded him for a moment, then said in a low, calm voice:

"I suppose I should try to undo what I've done now. I've got some first-aid stuff in my purse. If I can find it . . ." Kneeling before the boy who still rocked, she looked with anomalous tranquility at the place between his legs where she'd kicked him.

Denton took a long breath, relaxing from his paralysis, an actor between scenes.

He put a hand on Donna's shoulder, felt her stiffen beneath his touch. He put his hand in his pocket, asking, "Where did you go when they jumped me?"

"I hid in a doorwell. I thought they were after me. When I saw them surround you I went around to the other side of the alley and came through it, and up behind them."

She turned from him to face the boy. *"Why?"* she asked.

Through grated teeth the boy answered, "Hurzbau . . ."

The name made Denton realize where he had seen the
leader of the gang before: in the park, the boy who had asked
about his father under the generator. He stepped toward the
other tough, demanding, "Hurzbau *what?*"

"Hurzbau's father's in the hospital. Under the generator.
He made us do it. He's our packleader. He said you were a
vampire killing his father. He watched you, followed
you. . . ."

Donna screamed shortly, the cry becoming a sigh as Denton heard her body hit the concrete sidewalk even before he
turned around. A knife's black hilt protruded from her side,
stuck from the back by the boy who stood, wavering, ready to
fall, still coughing blood. Denton recognized Hurzbau's son,
and he wondered: *Why her instead of me?*

The boy collapsed, crumpling limply, blood sliding between
his skin and the transparent suit, the plastic making the blood
seem orange and artificial.

Denton felt empathic pain in his own side as, sobbing, he
ran to Donna. She was still breathing but unconscious. The
knife was in to the hilt. He was afraid to pull it out and perhaps
allow too much blood to escape.

"Here. Call an ambulance." The boy who had spoken before was standing, one hand still on his crotch, something like
regret in his face. He handed Denton a public pocket-fone.
Denton fumbled frantically to punch for EMERGENCY.

A small metallic voice responded, and he gave directions.
When he had done he looked up and down the street, wondering that it was so deserted after all the noise. There were
three bright street lights on the block. Denton, Donna, and the
remainder of the gang were visible and starkly outlined in the
pool of light under the crowded skyscraper apartments lining
both sides of the street.

The events of the past few minutes caught up with Denton
when he felt blood warming the hand resting on Donna's still
leg. He looked up at the boy who just stood there, face
blanked.

"All of you are going to regret this, kid," Denton said in what he hoped was a steely, uncompromising tone.

The boy just shrugged.

He couldn't go to work now, to watch a man die under a generator scoop knowing that Donna was dying under one just like it. He pondered the idea of quitting his job. Somehow he felt that losing his job at the generator would be a self-betrayal. It brought him a strange peace, as he sat in full health watching the patient wilt under the glass scoop like an ant burnt by a magnifying glass. Saying to himself: *I'm still strong, it passed me by.*

He decided not to go to work. He kept seeing Donna's name on the shift chart. They had expected *him* to tend her generator. No. No. He couldn't visit her, even, while off duty. She was in a coma. He had to get his mind off it. He hadn't slept at all that night and his eyes burned with exhaustion. He would go out and get something to eat and if Buxton decided to fire him because of his absence then the decision to leave the job would be made *for* him.

He walked through the hospital lobby and into the glaring sunshine reflecting off the white buildings of the hospital complex. A growing tension was surmounting his composure. But he was an actor so no one could tell.

Not even Alice. Alice was standing on the steps to the hospital, handing out pamphlets. She saw him immediately, seeing first the black uniform she hated, and then her once-lover interred inside.

Denton hoped to avoid her, but before he could turn away she ran to him and, thrusting a pamphlet in his hand, embraced him. He pulled away, embarrassed, feeling tension about to break loose. The glare seemed to intensify, magnifying glass hovering over the ant. Alice laughed.

"Still working there? I think you must really like your job, Ronnie."

His mouth worked but his lines wouldn't come. He shook his head and finally managed, "I'd like to talk to you about it.

Uh—welcome your opinion. But I've gotta go start my shift."
He turned and hurried back into the coolness of the hospital,
feeling her smug smile hanging on to the back of his neck.

It was suddenly important to him that he go to work. He
had nothing to expiate.

In the elevator, alone, he glanced at the crumpled pamphlet. He read:

". . . if it is inevitable that a man must die, let him do it
with dignity. Death has long been a gross national product,
especially since United States intervention in the Arab-Israeli
conflict. But a bullet through the heart kills quickly; death under the generator comes tediously. The common fallacy that
entropic generators promote death has been proven untrue,
but what do they do to ease or inhibit death? The presence of
a generator is psychologically damaging to the dying, causing
them to give up the fight for recovery before they normally
would . . ."

He remembered Hurzbau's words: *Can you say it doesn't
take away from my life if you don't know how it works?*

"Mr. Buxton? Can I talk to you?"

Hardly looking up, Buxton demanded, "Well? What are
you doing here? You were supposed to be in four-fifty-six
twenty minutes ago."

"I want you to explain the principles of the entropic generator to me. I think it's my responsibility to know."

"Oh hell," Buxton spat, disappointed, "is that all? Look it
up in the Encyclopedia Britannica."

"I did. It was all in jargon. And they told us briefly and
none too clearly when I was being trained for this job. But I
never really cared to understand till now. But a . . . friend
of mine is under—"

"Under the generator, right? And *now* you want to know.
I've heard that one before too many times. Okay, Denton. I'll
explain. Once. And you are going to be docked for the time it
takes me to explain and the time you weren't working."

Denton shrugged, sat down across from Buxton. He felt like a boy going to confession.

Buxton sighed and began, playing with a pencil as he spoke: "The word *entropy,* literally translated, means *turning toward energy.* From our relative viewpoint we usually define entropy as the degree of disorder in a substance. Entropy always increases and available energy diminishes. So it seems. From our point of view, when we see someone's system of order decaying it seems as if the growth of entropy means a drop of energy. It appears that something is going away from us." He paused to organize his thoughts, began to doodle on scratchpaper.

Denton tapped his fingers irritably. "Yeah? So what? When people die they lose energy—"

"No, they don't lose it in the sense we're concerned with, and SHUT UP AND LISTEN because I'm not going to explain this to you twice. This is already the fourth time this month I've had to go through all this. . . . Now, when you get old, your eyesight fails so it appears as if you see less and less all the time. Things in this world are blotting out, blurring up. Actually, you're seeing something more than you could see before your eyesight failed. When your eyesight dims your entropy-sight increases. Objects look that way, blurred and graylike, in the other dimension, because they possess a form defined by where they are *not* rather than where they *are.*"

"What dimension?"

Denton was lost.

"The dimension manifested concurrent with the accruence of entropy. We used to think entropy undid creation and form, but in its total sense, entropy creates a form so obverse to ours that it appears not to be there. It creates in a way we don't really understand but which we've learned to use." He cleared his throat, embarrassed by his lapse into erudition. "Anyway, the universe is constantly shifting dimensions. From entropic focus to our type of order and back again. When you get old and seem to be feeling and hearing and seeing less, you are actually perceiving the encroachment of that other universe."

They were silent for five breaths. The taciturn old Jew tapped his pencil agitatedly.

Denton wondered if his inability to comprehend stemmed from his youth. He wasn't decayed enough yet.

"What I'm trying to say," Buxton went on wearily, "is that entropy is a progression instead of a regression. When someone is walking past you it seems like they're regressing, in a relative way, because they are walking toward where you have already been, to what is behind you. But to them, they are *pro*gressing. There are two kinds of known energy, on a cosmic scale: electrical-nuclear energy causing form, and the negative energy of antiform. Nothing is really lost when you die. What occurs is a trade."

"You mean like water displacement? Going into *there*, some of it is forced into *here?*"

"More or less. The generators change the energy of death into usable electric power."

"But if you take energy from a dying person, doesn't that make them die faster?"

"WILL YOU PAY ATTENTION, FOR GOD'S SAKE!" Buxton was determined to get through. "*No*. It doesn't take anything from a dying person. It accumulates energy that's radiated as a result of dying. The negative energy is released into the inanimate environment whether the generator is there or not. The scoop doesn't come into contact with the patient himself . . . it reacts only to the side-effect of his biological dissolution." He took a deep breath. "The main idea is that entropy is not the lack of something, not a subtraction, but an addition. We learned how to tap it because the energy crisis forced us to put up with the temporary discomfort—purely psychological and rather silly—of having the scoop directly over a dying person. When it comes my time to go, I'll be damn proud to contribute something. None of my life is wasted that way, not even its end. One individual causes a remarkable amount of negative energy to be radiated as he dies, you know. We've only been using it practically for five years and there are still a lot of things we don't understand about it."

"So why do it to people? Why not plants?"

"Because various organisms have variegated patterns of radiating negative energy. We don't know how to tap all of them yet. We can do it with cattle and people now. We're working on plants."

"I don't know, I, uh . . ." Denton stumbled over his words, knowing that Buxton would be infuriated by the objection. "But couldn't a generator damage the morale of a person dying? Make him believe it's too late and prematurely give up? I mean, susceptibility to disease is largely psychological, and if you're under pressure by being under the scoop—" He cut short, swallowing, seeing Buxton's growing anger.

Hot ashes sprayed from Buxton's wagging pipe as he spoke. "Denton, all that is a lot of conjectural hogwash. And it is pure stupidity to babble about it in the face of the worst energy crisis the world has ever known. We may have the energy problem licked forever if we can learn to draw negative energy from the dying of plants and small animals and such. But people like you might just ruin that hope. And I want you to know, Denton, that I'm going to seriously consider letting you go, so if you don't want to clinch my decision you'd better get the hell to—"

"I can't go to my assigned shift, sir. I know the girl under that scoop."

"Okay then, that leaves Durghemmer. Take it or no more job."

Feeling drained, Denton nodded dumbly and left the office.

Durghemmer could wait. Denton called hospital information and was informed that Donna was still unconscious.

Denton went to see his only close friend. He took the bus to Glennway Park.

Donald Armor was a cripple in one sense and completely mobile in another. He had been a pro race-car driver for six years, several times taking national honors. During the final lap of the 1983 Indy 500 (the last one before the race was outlawed), while in second place, Armor's car spun out and bounced off the car behind it and went into the grandstands, killing five onlookers, maiming four. When gas-cars were banned and electric air-cars instituted in 1986, the authorities made an exception in Armor's case. He was allowed to drive his own car, the only vehicle on the streets with wheels, because he could drive nothing else. Part of the firewall of the racing car had been ripped loose by the impact of the accident, slashing deep into Armor's side, partially castrating him on the way and cracking his spine. Doctors could not remove the shred without killing him.

Armor was a rich man and he had a car built around him, customized to his specifications. It was a small sports car, but with the cockpit, firewall, steering wheel, and dashboard of the original Indy racer. He was now a permanent organ of the vehicle, living in it day and night, unable and unwilling to leave. Until he died. Excreting through a colostomy bag, eating at drive-ins, he was aware of the absurdity of his existence but he considered his predicament appropriate to the society in which he lived.

Denton sat in the seat next to Armor and, as usual, tried not to look at the thirteen inches of ragged steel protruding for the driver's right side to run to a ball-joint connecting him with the dashboard. The ball-joint gave him limited freedom within the car.

Armor had rudimentary use of his scarred and twisted legs, enough to gun the car down the boulevard with a speed and fluidity which never failed to amaze Denton. Armor drove without hesitation or false starts, always twenty miles in excess of the speed limit, knowing that no policeman would give him a ticket. They all knew him. Armor was famous, and he was dying. He had less than a year to live (long-range complications of the accident) but they could never install a generator over a moving car. He was the source of livelihood for some reporters who spent all their time trying to get interviews and photographs of him. He had no comforts; no radio or tape deck or juice dispensers. He didn't drink and he couldn't have sex.

"What's eating you today, Ron?" Armor asked in a voice like the distant rumble of a semitruck. He was dark and rawboned and his bushy black brows sprouted alone on a scarred bald head. His hard gray eyes were perpetually lost in the spaces between the white dashes marking the abdomen of the road. "Something's messing you up," he said.

They had been friends since before Armor's accident. Armor knew Denton almost as well as he knew the road. Denton told him about Donna and his doubts concerning the generator.

Armor listened without comment. His eyes didn't leave the road—they rarely did—and his features remained expressionless aside from slight intensifications when the road called for more concentration.

Denton concluded, "And I can't bring myself to leave the job. Donna is still in the coma, so I can't talk to her about it. I almost feel like I'm working against her by continuing there. I know it's irrational. . . ."

"What is it you like so much that you can't quit?"

"It's not that. I . . . well, jobs aren't easy to find."

"I know where you can get another job."

He eased the car to a halt. They were parked in front of TREMMER AND FLEISHER SLAUGHTERING/PROCESSING. Below the older sign was, newly painted in black: GENERATOR ANNEX.

"My brother Harold works here," Armor said. He hadn't turned off the engine. He rarely did. "He remembers you. He can get you a job here. Go on up to the personnel office. That's where he works. You might like this job better than the other, I imagine." He turned uncompromising eyes from the hood of the car and looked at Denton with a five-hundred-horsepower gaze.

"Okay." Denton shrugged. "Anything you say. I can't go back to work now anyway." He opened the car door and got out, feeling his back painfully uncramping after the restriction of the bucket seat. He looked through the open door. Armor was still watching him.

"I'll wait here," Armor said with finality.

The bright light hurt Denton's eyes as he followed Harold Armor, brother to Donald, into a barnlike aluminum building labeled SLAUGHTERHOUSE GENERATOR ANNEX I.

Inside, the sibilance of air-conditioners was punctuated with long bestial sighs from dying cattle. There were two long rows of stalls, a bubble of the generator scoop completely enclosing each prostrate steer. The top of each scoop ducted into a thick vitreous cable joining others from adjoining stalls in a network of silvery wire like a spiderweb canopy overhead.

"Now these cattle here—well, some of 'em are cows what got old—they have a generator for the whole lot of 'em, and one compensator for every three animals," Harold intoned proudly. "And we've got some we've maintained there at just the right level of decay, you know, for six to eight months. And that's just plain difficult. They die a lot on us, though. A lot of 'em dying of old age. Most of 'em we bleed to death."

"You bleed them?" Denton was unable to conceal his horror. Seeing Denton's reaction, Harold stiffened defensively.

"Damn right we do. How else can we keep them at the right level of decay and still keep them alive long enough to produce? Sure, I know what you're going to ask. Everyone does when they first come here. The government shut the ASPCA up because of the power shortage. And of course part of your job as compensator here is you'll have to learn how to adjust their bleeding and feeding so they die at the right speed. It's a bit more work than at the hospital, where they die for you naturally. But it pays more than at the hospital. All you have to remember is that if they sneak back up on you and recover too much, you either have to bleed them more or feed them less. Sometimes we poison them some too, when they first come here, to get them on their way."

Denton stood by one of the cells and observed a fully

grown bull with ten-inch horns, massive rib cage rising and falling irregularly, eyes opening and closing and opening and closing. . . .

"Now *that* one," Harold droned, "hasn't been here but a week and he ain't used to it yet. Most of them just lay there and forget they're alive after a few weeks or so. See, you can see marks on the stall where he's been kicking it and his hoof is bleeding—we'll have to patch that up, we don't want him to get an infection. Die too soon that way. You can see he's going to come along good cuz his coat is gettin' rough and fur startin' to come off. . . ."

The trapped beast looked at Denton with dulled eyes devoid of fear. It was lying on its side, head lolling from the stall opening. Three thick plastic tubes were clamped with immovable iron bands to its sagging neck. The steer seemed to be in transition between instinctual rebellion and capitulation. Intermittently it twitched and lifted its head a few inches, as if trying to recall how to stand.

From the New York *Times* review of Ronald Denton's only play, *All Men Are Created Sequels:*
". . . like all so-called absurdism, Denton's play was an inert corpse albeit a charming one. This state of inflexible down beat was probably intentional, and so, like all cadavers, the play began to decay well before the second act, as perhaps it was supposed to. By the end of the second act, the stage was a figurative miasma of putrid flesh, squirming with parasitic irrelevancies. The least Mr. Denton could have done would have been the courtesy of a generator scoop hooked up to the audience so that we could glean something of value from the affair as the audience died of boredom."

Denton was looking out the window, wondering at the gall Armor had exhibited in arranging for him to see the slaughterhouse. He had known—
Durghemmer interrupted his thoughts.
"Come here, kid!"

Denton didn't want to go around to the other side of the generator. He didn't want to look at Durghemmer.

"*Comere,* boy!"

Denton sighed and stood up. "Yes?"

Durghemmer's face was round and robust. His eyes were bright buttons sewn deep in the hollows over his cheeks. He had a miniature round mouth, a wisp of white hair, and minimal chin. His jowls shook when he laughed. He pointed at Denton with a stubby finger. "You skeered of something, kid?"

"Shouldn't you be asleep, Mr. Durghemmer? It's past nine."

"Shouldn't *you* be asleep, kid? Sleep?" He laughed shrilly, cowbells filtering through the plastic bell of the scoop. He half sat up, grimaced, fell back.

Emanuel Durghemmer had come to the hospital three years before, dying of meningitis. He had been too far along for help; they had expected him to die within a week. A generator was immediately placed over him. He went into a month-long coma. When he woke, the needles jumped. According to the meters, he had come a substantial step closer to death by regaining consciousness. And according to hospital legend, he had sat up directly upon awakening from the coma, and *laughed.* The generator again had registered a drop in lifeforce and a corresponding gain in entropic energy. Each week for three years Durghemmer had shown signs of being on the verge of death. Always in pain, he delivered more negative energy than any other individual in the hospital. And he had developed a corrosive bedridden manner to counteract the doctors' bedside manners.

Denton was disquieted by Durghemmer's paradoxical joviality. But Denton had two hours left of his shift. He decided to make the most of it, find out what he could.

Somehow Durghemmer's attitude made Donna's imminent death seem ludicrous.

"You're wondering, aren't you?" Durghemmer asked, as if he were still a politician casting rhetoric. "You're wondering how I stay alive."

"No. I don't give a damn."

"But you do. You care for the simplest of reasons. You know you're going to die someday and you wonder how long you'll last under the generator and what it will be like watching the needle go up and down. Or maybe—if it's not you, is it someone else? Someone close to you dying, kid?"

No surprise that Durghemmer knew. The old parasite had been in the hospital for three years, a record by two and a half years for being under the generator. He could smell death a long way away.

"All right, but so what?" Denton said impulsively. "So you're right. It's girl friend."

"She got cancer between the legs?" Hollow laughter reverberated inside the scoop. Lines of mirth on the old man's face meshed indistinguishably with lines of pain.

Denton wanted to smash the plastic of the scoop to get at the old politician's sour mouth with his fist. Instead, he said coolly: "No. She was knifed. I've got to see her. I heard she came around for a while this afternoon. Maybe I can . . ." He shrugged. "I've got to explain things."

"May as well write her off, kid. Nobody but me has ever figured out how to use it. I had training when I was mayor." He guffawed, coughing phlegm.

"What did you do to Burt Lemmer?"

"That kid that resigned? He was a short spit, only on my generator three weeks. Usually takes them at least a month." He closed his eyes. In a low, tense voice: "You know, sometimes pain sharpens things for you. It kind of wakes you up and makes you see better. You ever notice when your gut hurts and you feel like every sound and sight is too loud or bright for you to stand it? Everything makes you feel sicker because you're seeing it so well, so clearly. Sometimes people who haven't done anything with their lives become good painters when they get sick because the hurt *makes* them look at things. And sometimes—" He drifted off for a full minute, his eyes in limbo. Then he spoke conspiratorially, whispering more to himself than to Denton, "Sometimes I see things in the blossoms of pain. Useful things. Peeks into that other world. I go into it a little ways, then I come back here and I'm on solid ground. And I see these invisible wires connecting each man to the others, like puppet strings all mixed up."

Denton had lost interest in the old man's ramblings. He could see Donna's eyes smoldering with pain like the red dials of the generator.

Durghemmer's generator hummed into life as it began to absorb a flood of negative energy. The old man was tiring. The machine began to chuckle to itself. Durghemmer lay composed, a faint smile lost in the mazelike etchings of his face.

"Durghemmer," Denton said, standing. "I've got to see that woman. I've got to make sure she's all right. Now look, if I go, would you refrain from calling the nurse when I go out unless it's an absolute emergency? I've *got* to—"

"Okay, kid. But you can write off your girl friend. She hasn't lived long enough to learn. . . ." He had spoken without bothering to open his eyes.

Denton was alone with Donna; he had bribed the scheduled compensator. He peered through the scoop at her nervously, irrationally afraid that she might already be dead. Her elfin features, unconscious, blinked in and out of shadow with the strobing of the generator lights in the darkened room. Denton checked the dials, rechecked them, found a compensating factor he had missed the first time. He adjusted the intake of the scoop.

She was dropping. The needles were climbing.

He flipped on the intercom, walked around to the other side of the bed. "Donna? Can you hear me?" He glanced at the meter. It jumped. She was coming around but it took strength from her to awaken. Maybe talking to her would make her weak, perhaps cause her death, he thought abruptly. Something he should have considered sooner. His heart was a fist pounding the bars of his chest.

Her eyes opened, silver-blue platinum, metal tarnished with desperation.

He spoke hastily: "I'm sorry about everything, Donna. I don't know how you got involved in my problems. . . ." He waved his hands futilely.

She looked at him without comprehension for a moment, then recognition cleared her eyes.

"I shouldn't bother you now," he added gratuitously, "but I had to talk to you."

It came to him that he really had no idea what he wanted to say.

"Get out of here, Ron . . . you came for yourself, not for me." Her voice was thin as autumn ice. And like being awakened with ice-water, Denton was shocked into realization: It was true, he had been more worried about his own feelings than hers.

"You came here to apologize. Big deal. Maybe you should apologize to that Hurzbau kid. I heard that he died. I'm not moralizing. We killed him together." Her eyes fluttered.

"Donna?" She was giving up. Her voice trailed off. Get her attention, make her fight her way back. He buzzed for the nurse and shouted, *"Donna!"* His voice stretched wiry from hysteria.

She opened her eyes a crack and murmured, "They took a psychological test for you, didn't they? They tested you and knew you were right for the job."

The nurse bustled in then and Denton pressed the green button that lifted the scoop.

As he left he saw the needles, still rising. Rapaciously, the generator giggled.

He shuffled with great effort through the halls, two days' lack of sleep catching up to him. His arms and legs seemed to be growing softer, as if his bones were dissolving. He came to the window overlooking the parking lot. As he expected, Armor was waiting for him below, driving around and around and around without pausing, circling the parking lot in a loop of abeyance.

Denton left the window. He couldn't face Armor now. He

scuffled down the antiseptic hallways. He fancied that he felt
negative energy radiating from him like a dark halo. The
penumbra grew darker as he sank deeper into exhaustion.
His throat contracted till he could hardly breathe. He had
memorized the exact shape of the trickle of blood on
Donna's chin, the last thing that had caught his attention before the nurse had made him leave. It had runneled down
from her nose onto her cheek, splitting into forks, a dark
lightning bolt. He pictured the fine branchings of red multi-
plying in the atmosphere around him as if the air were filled
with a skein of ethereal blood veins. The red lines connected
the spectral orderlies and nurses rushing past, like the wires
Durghemmer had described connecting the heads of everyone
in the city. Denton walked slowly, plowing through molten
wax to Durghemmer's room.

"I want to *know,* Durghemmer, "he said to the old man, as
he entered the sterile chamber. "I know you steal the negative
energy of the scoop for yourself. I want to know *how.*"

The old man grinned toothlessly. His gums were cracked
and dried, making his mouth into the crumbling battlements
of a ruined city. He sat up, and the needles rose again.

Denton leaned wearily on the generator, determined to
come to terms with death.

"I figured you'd want to know, Denton." Durghemmer
laughed, moths tumbling dustily in his throat. "I can see just
by looking at you that the girl died."

Denton nodded. The movement might have been made by a
scarecrow swayed by a breeze.

"Sure, lad, I'll show you just how I thrive in this hole. I'll
show you how I keep an even keel under this scoop like a
pheasant under glass. I'll show you just exactly and honest to
God. You just watch me now."

"Watch you? You mean I can *see* how you do it?"

"Sure. You just watch now."

The dark room seemed to congeal with grains of opacity.
The generator hummed happily to itself. Denton leaned for-

ward, hands on the control panel, tired eyes locked desperately onto Durghemmer.

The decaying politician lay back and folded his hands on his chest. Then, he began to chuckle.

Denton was completely baffled. As far as he could see, the old man was doing nothing at all . . .

. . . except laughing.

In the long voyages between stars, people are going to need psychological safeguards to protect their sanity: strict rules, carefully planned recreations. Because a starship is a self-enclosed prison amid light-years of empty blackness—and there will be no escape if something goes wrong, and madness invades such a ship.

GLENN CHANG *is a young man from Hawaii who now lives in Oregon. He's another Clarion alumnus, but he'd sold his first story (to* If *Magazine) before attending Clarion.*

Stars and Darkness

BY GLENN CHANG

"Dying, we live," I say, raising the scalpel. "Living, we only see pain. Isn't that right, Yamada?"

I look down at Yamada. Beneath my other hand, his body spasms in agony.

"Stop it, Yang," he says. His words are barely intelligible. "Stop it."

"But I don't want to," I say. "And neither would you want me to. Not really." I reach up and grasp his face. "Sweet pain, Yamada. Do you feel it? Does it send you into fits of ecstasy? Jar you into new heights of awareness? It should, if what your 'confidential' file says is true. Repressed masochism, if I recall correctly. Is that right, Yamada? Are you a repressed masochist?"

I squeeze his jaw suddenly, and I can feel the broken crowns of his teeth rip the inside of his check. A tortured gurgle escapes his lips.

I straighten. "So. You are not. You do not cry, 'Yes, Yes, it is beautiful.' Because it is not. Life is not beautiful for you, Yamada. All it holds for you is ugliness."

I bring my face close to his and the blade of the scalpel to his chest. "Then perhaps I should end it for you," I whisper, slowly moving the blade in circles on his skin, leaving fine lines that well into thick trails of blood. "I will end your miserable life. Because I hate you, Yamada. I always have. Nothing would please me more than to see you dead, your body hang:ng from its heels on meathooks and your throat cut, standing by like a side of beef to be quartered." I raise the scalpel and bring it behind his ear. His body struggles, but the straps hold him tight; I hold his head steady with my other hand.

"Please," he manages to say, almost sobbing. "Enough. End this, Yang. Please."

"All right," I say softly, "I will. Now." And I plunge the scalpel in, and jerk it in an arc, and his life spills out in a bubbling crimson stream, and I close my eyes and feel the gratification slipping over me, carrying me into sweet unconsciousness—

Until I open them again and see that I am awake.

As usual, I am first. I blink several times and stare upward through the clear viewplate at the featureless ceiling. Then the sensors note that I am fully conscious, and I hear the hiss of the lid rising, and I clamber out of the foam-lined coffin, naked and trembling, the sensor disks popping off my skin and the cords hanging over the edges.

I look at myself and see my skin shiny with sweat. As usual. It takes a few minutes to get my breathing down to normal and my legs steady. I glance at the other pod and see Yamada there, still asleep—and unmarked. And alive. I shudder involuntarily and step through the short corridor to the shower stall.

The warm water is good on my skin, washing off the sweat and the dregs of dreams and guilt. The cycle is finished when I am finished, and the blasts of warm air dry me quickly. I find my suit and slip it on.

When I reenter the dream-room, Yamada is awake, sitting

on the side of his pod, still nude. His eyes when he looks at me are full of fear and hatred. Like all the others before. I ignore him, and walk over to the indicator panels.

"How many shall we say went through it this time?" I ask, my back to him, reaching for the microcircuit boards. "Ten? Twelve?"

"You bastard," Yamada says. His voice quavers, barely under control.

"Let's say twelve. A little more—there." I replace the circuit board with the proper jimmied one, then walk along the other ten pods designated, reaching under the controls on each one and adjusting them.

I walk back toward him, trying not to look at him, though I can feel his eyes on me. He tries to stand, finds himself unsteady, and quickly sits down again.

"Why?" he asks, breathing hard. "What reason is there to hate me?"

I stop and look at him. "None that I know of," I say patiently. "You know that. Some deep-rooted reason, obscure or ridiculous to our conscious minds, that I cannot get at because it's hidden by guilt, or self-disgust, or the like. The dream-machine is the only thing that can reach beyond these layers, to the subconscious, to our deepest urges. But ask me what these urges are—" I spread my hands outward. "As well ask me how it felt to be born."

"But—" he stammers. "But we should try to uncover these feelings, to cure them. The flight depends on our cooperation, our—our survival. If one of us is sick—"

"Oh? And how would you tell the others you discovered one of us was sick? By violating the Rules, and by using the machine for a dual rather than in a group, without the guidance of a Stable? No. If we want to keep using it for our purposes, we must keep silent. You know the penalty for breaking any Rule; do you want to end up as fertilizer for the hydroponics tanks?"

Yamada shakes his head. "I don't understand," he says, his

voice plaintive. "It wasn't like I thought it would be. Not at all."

I shrug. "That's the risk you take. It all depends on whose is the more dominant personality. And whose is weaker."

Yamada stares downward, his face rigid. "I won't do it again," he says with determination.

"Oh, you will," I say, turning to leave. I stop to give him a parting word. "You'll come back. You'll do this over and over again—because one of these times *you* might be able to kill *me*." Then I leave.

It is the machine that keeps us sane. It takes our minds off the long trip, releases the emotions and frustrations that build up, in ways that the tapes, or the prescribed mental exercises, or the recreational games never could. All those things are for the limited, the weak-minded. But the dreams, the worlds the machine leads us to . . . how can anything compare with them?

But the others don't know. They can't understand. They stay in their safe, ineffectual little activities. Like Sedjayev and Pruitt, playing their silly fugue-chess games at every leisure period.

"Back two milliseconds," Pruitt says.

"Up four minutes." Sedjayev moves his dial.

"Hmm, let's . . . no. All right. Up two." Pruitt studies the tallies closely.

"Two back."

"Up three."

"Back five." They hunch forward, eager and feral.

"Up six—no, I mean—"

"Too late. Coalescence and fugue." The board glows red and tallies the points for Sedjayev. He smiles and leans back, basking in his victory.

I sneer at them both. "Stupid," I say. "Stupid games you play. Why bother wasting your time with this?"

But they ignore me, as they always do. Well, let them. Let them all.

I look around the recreation chambers, at the others trying
to relax. McAdams putters with the synthetron; Hadig reviews
the theater tapes; and, here, and there, they recline, chatter,
play the games, and stare up at the ceiling in their private
musings. And how many more occupy the bedchambers—
how many couples lie beyond those innocuous metal doors,
grasping at each other in their fumbling sweaty embraces?

Simpleminded pursuits. Animal passions. They are unthink-
ing sheep. I despise them all.

I see Yamada before a game console, working the controls
with a tight-lipped frustration. I go over to him.

"Hello, Yamada," I say. "Trying to relax? Easing your
mind?"

His hands jerk, startled; he looks up at me, then at the
board, then curses and strikes it with his fist. But the screen is
quite strong—protected by transparent duraplast—and
remains unharmed. The glow from the word ERROR filling the
screen continues to bathe Yamada's face.

"Stupid game," he mutters. "Stupid. Like everything else
here."

"That's right," I say. "Good that you've finally realized it.
Better that than the mindless existence these others lead."

I reach out to him, but he spins out of my grasp and faces
me.

"The others. Yes, what about the others?" His expression is
a mixture of rage and frustration. "Must I stand apart? Must I
always remain aloof? Isn't there a way I can be closer to
them?"

"Not if they continue to be blind to the truth."

"Truth? What do *you* mean when you say 'truth'? *This
flight* is the truth. We're here on this ship for a purpose; we
have to face that. In order for the mission to succeed, we need
to maintain balance and harmony, and to cooperate—"

"Don't tell me about this mission." I speak with contempt.
"They've fooled us all, putting us on a journey to nowhere.
Where does this flight take us? Do you know? Does anyone?

No, only the Stables. They're our gods, ruling our lives, our sleeping hours, even—yes, even our dreams. And we obey them, oh so meekly and without question.

"But no more. Not if we become aware. Like me. And you. And the others before you. We don't have to follow their orders anymore. We can do as we please. Isn't that better than before, Yamada?" I lean close to him, grinning, with that last question.

He stands up abruptly, backing away from me. "I don't know—I have to think." His hands flutter in agitation, and he glances at the floor, his head jerking back and forth nervously. "I have to—to—" But he doesn't finish—only leaves the recreation chambers, all the others staring after him.

"Yes, Yamada," I say. "Think. But not for long. You'll be back." And I laugh out loud, and don't care whether they stare at me or not.

The flight. The great metal idol of the Ship. The hallowed Rules. Of what importance are they to me? To any of us? Here we sit in the Ship's swollen belly, held in gestation until it sees fit to give us forth in birthing when we reach the end of our journey. And where will it end? We don't know. The all-powerful directors haven't deemed us worthy of that information. Final destination, calculated flight time—all that is locked in nonretrievable memory cores. And in the memories of the Stables.

They are our surrogate directors, these Stables. They assign our tasks, schedule our hours, adjust our leisure periods, correlate our data—moving us about like robots in a shadow play, while they hide their tank-grown bodies behind code-locked doors and govern us from the safety of their vats.

Our only refuge is the dream-sessions. There we can let our fantasies come to life—but only if they are safe, and harmless, and able to be integrated with those of the others in the session. And even here we are all under the careful watch of a Stable.

Careful watch, indeed. How laughable that is—that a blob of gray matter, floating in nutrient juices and with a hundred sensory wires trailing from it, could have the capacity to observe and understand us. *That* is what makes our Rules. *That* is what we have to answer to for any violations. Maintain the balance, it tells us—the homeostasis necessary for optimum probability of success of mission. Any upsetting factor will be eliminated; any deviant crew member goes into the tanks. The safety of the flight is all-important.

How I despise them.

If they only knew what really goes on. But they don't—and they never will, as long as I continue to take the necessary precautions with every dual I undertake. There are only a few of us now. But eventually I will indoctrinate all the crew members—and make them all dependent on me. No longer will I have to endure their contempt—people like Lopez, and Andresen, and Mogotu, sitting there at mealtime, sipping their fizz and ignoring me. Me.

"Words associate, feelings culminate," says Lopez.

"We wait, not late, for the bait at eight," says Andresen in turn.

"Come sit by the furnace with your feet in your ears," Mogotu says triumphantly, falling off his chair, and they all convulse into laughter.

Yamada and I sit at the next table—I quiet and serene, he morose and pensive on my left.

I lean over and whisper, "Perk up, my friend. Let the fizz work. Enjoy. Have fun. Live your life to the fullest."

He swirls his glass of fizz, still untouched, and stares into it. "How can I when I died the other day?"

"No matter. It'll probably happen again. Besides, it's only a dream, isn't it?"

"But it was real—so real. I could feel the pain, and my life just ebbing away. I—" He abruptly brings the glass to his lips, but changes his mind and lowers it.

"You can always decide to stop," I say.

He looks at me for several seconds. "I won't stop," he says. His voice is low and flat. "Not until I get you. And I will, someday."

"What is this, Yamada?" calls Lopez from the other table. "Talking to yourself again, eh?"

Yamada's head jerks in the direction of the others, then he curses, rises suddenly, and stalks off.

"Oh ho," Lopez says, eyes wide to mock surprise. "The delicate one."

Their rude laughter fills the dining chamber, but I say nothing and sip my drink. Go on, I think. Ignore me. You won't be blind long. Your time will come.

Later, Yamada pleads with me to undertake yet another dual session.

"No," I say. "It's too soon for you. You've hardly recovered from the first one. Look at yourself. See how badly it's affected you."

"Damn you," he shouts, his voice ringing along the corridor. He lowers his voice and says, "You owe this to me. You owe me another chance."

"In time," I say. "Do you think you're the only one? There were others before you."

"What do I care about them? It's *my* chance I'm talking about." His words become more and more vehement.

"That bad?" I say, feigning concern. "The dull life of the Ship routine getting to you? The larger sessions too tame?"

"Yes. Yes!"

"Poor, unbalanced Yamada," I say, shaking my head. "You're no different from the others. Don't you see? All of you have these basic weaknesses that can only be satisfied in an unrestricted fantasy. It was so simple to pick you out during the normal sessions. But you'll do everything my way, or not at all, for I hold the key."

Yamada mutters something, then suddenly lunges at me. But I quickly sidestep him, and he whirls to face me, breathing hard.

"Watch it, friend," I say. "I can easily deny you any time at all."

"What's to stop me from trying it with someone else?" he says with barely controlled fury.

"The fact that only I know how to readjust the settings. I'm your only partner. Keep that in mind, till the next time. If there is one." And I turn and walk away.

What fools they all are! What arrogance they have! Yamada is no different. They all feel that way—superior, stronger, full of conceit. There is no outlet for them to display their bright qualities, except for the duals I set up. How easy it is to appeal to their vanity, then to turn their dreams back on them by playing on their hidden fears. I can only think of them with contempt, and it is with contempt that I treat them, until, in the end, there is nothing left to do but kill them.

"Flex," I say, pulling the cord tighter around her neck. "Move your hips—faster now. Yes, that's it."

I watch the muscles spasm in Fletcher's back and the shuddering in her splayed buttocks as I pump myself in and out, methodically carrying out the sodomy. I slide one hand over her slick skin, lingering over the swell of her breast, her soft side, and the curve of her hip. With the other I jerk up the cord, and her face twists to the side. It is mottled blue, and her tongue hangs out of her mouth. I can hear her trying to gag.

"Scream," I say, thrusting hard. "Cry out. Let me hear your pain." I feel something give, and I know that I have torn her inside. "Isn't this what you've dreamed of? What you've wondered about? This must be truly exciting for you, Fletcher."

No answer. I shrug and renew my efforts, until her final choking gurgle comes, and I come, and then I release the cord and smile at her bloated face, the eyes open and staring.

When we wake, she is inarticulate with rage and hatred.

"*Kill you*," she screams, teeth bared. Her fingers swoop for my eyes. "Kill you for that. Filth. Pervert."

I grab her hands and bend her back over the pod, holding her immobile with my body. "You had your chance in the session," I say. "What kind of perversions did you have in mind for me? What kind of grisly death would I have undergone? Look to your own mind first for the signs of sickness."

I release her and step back. She still glares at me, but does not attack.

"Don't give me that," she says. "You're the one who's sick. I should report you—"

"And yourself? And all the others? No. They won't punish me alone."

"This isn't worth it," she says, shaking her head. "It's not what I want." She looks at me accusingly. "All because of you. You twist around everything to the way you want it. You give us nothing of what we want."

"Just a case of the dominant mind assuming control. If you want your world, you have to work for it. Be thankful you have the chance to try at all." I rise and turn to leave. "Now, if you'll excuse me, I'm tired."

They are becoming bothersome, those like Fletcher and Yamada. I can feel their eyes watching me all the time, even in the crowds at leisure or mealtime. They sit together and whisper, casting glances my way. Or they accost me in the deserted corridors or between portals, begging for another dual. It has become an addiction for them; the dream-sessions are their only desire. How pitiful to watch them degrade themselves.

It has become so bothersome that I must escape their pawing advances from time to time, to go where it is quiet and I can be alone. Down below the living quarters, among the catwalks running alongside the food tanks and the humming energy converters—no one goes there except the technicians, checking the dials twice every shift. It is restful here; the only sounds are the purring of machinery and the whispers of my soles along the floor.

But I am not alone this time. Ahead of me, someone bends over the indicator dials, jotting down figures on her tally sheet. I don't recognize who it is in the darkness, until her face is illumined by the glow from a panel— Ah. It is one of us.

I walk up to her and stop. "I see they keep you busy, Hotaling," I say. "Not an exciting task they've selected you for, is it?"

Hotaling continues to record the readings as if I weren't there.

"Don't play coy games," I say, suddenly angry. "I know you too well."

She looks up, then at me, as if for the first time. Finally she says, "Who are you? I don't recall seeing you in the dining hall."

"And the sessions? Our duals? I suppose you don't remember those, either?" I am shouting at her now.

"Sessions? What are you talking about?" Genuine puzzlement appears on her face. "Who are you?" she says again, stepping toward me. "What is your station? Your job?"

"I don't have to tell you that," I say. "What my job is is my concern . . ." But my voice trails off, as I suddenly think: Job? What is my job? I must have one. But what is it?

No good. I can't remember.

I back away from her. "Sorry," I say. "My error. I mistook you for someone else."

"Wait," she says, walking faster. "What did you mean—"

But I turn and run away from her, away from her calls, and I don't slow down until they have long faded away.

One hundred twenty-eight crew members. Sessions held every forty hours, in rotating groups of ten or more. There are eight of us altogether. The others: Lee, Ostermeyer, Macombray, Sedjayev, Fletcher, Yamada. And Hotaling. I am sure of it.

Yet Hotaling does not remember. Is she deceiving me? But

her ignorance seems authentic. Could it be possible I imagined a dual with her?

And there is myself. Why can't I remember my job, even now? Surely I have one. But on the other hand, I can remember a dual with Hotaling that might not even have taken place.

I don't know what it means.

It doesn't matter. All is lost. I am discovered.

Stupid Yamada. All his fault, wanting another session long before he was ready. But so insistent I gave in just to be rid of him. So it went thus:

He was stronger than before, much stronger. Driven by vengeance perhaps, surely by madness. And this time *he* forced his world on *me*.

I parried a sword blow, just in time, though its force knocked me to the ground. I looked up to see him ready to plunge the bayonet in. I rolled out of the way; the long steel blade sank into the ground next to me. I got to my feet, facing him, and ducked under the whistling steel net. I flattened to the ground again and felt the wind from his battleax as it arced through the space where my head had been.

I felt anger and frustration. This was what they all must have felt before. Now it was happening to me, and I didn't like it.

"Enough," I said, furious. "This must stop."

Yamada's face wore a death's-head grin. "The words I said last time," he said. "But now from you." He began whirling the bolo in his hand. "All right. I'll end it. The way you did for me." He hurled the bolo and moved forward, a dagger appearing in his other hand.

But I moved quickly, ducking under again, and appeared behind him. A kick, and he dropped the dagger, then to his knees. I grasped him about the neck. All the surging passions —anger, fear, hatred—seemed to overwhelm me.

"Die," I said, clubbing him with my fist. "Die. Die." My words became shouts, then incoherent screams in time with my blows smashing his teeth, his nose, cracking the cheek-bones and the jutting jaw, turning his face into shapeless pulp. Over and over I struck him, my first rising, falling, rising—

I sit up against the open pod, my arm upraised, sweating and gasping for air. The sudden coolness is like a shock against my skin. The heavy silence screams at me.

I look at Yamada's pod. The cover is ajar. His hand juts out from under it.

I walk over to it, lift the cover, and look down at him. Into his open staring eyes, wide with—horror? shock? surprise? The muscles are twisted as if in agony. His body is arched and stiff. I check his pulse and respiration. He is dead.

"In there. I heard a shout." The voice comes from outside. I hear fumbling at the locked door.

I look here and there wildly. What to do? Where to hide? I try behind a pod. No good. No room.

"Come on, get it open."

"I'm trying, damnit. Somebody's put on the triple security lock." Now I hear a babble of voices, many people trying to get in.

There, behind the console. I squeeze through the space behind the metal shelf, mindful of the metal leads and the sharp edges against my skin. I press my back against the wall, sticking as if my perspiration were glue.

"Okay, it's open." I hear the door slide, and the voices now in full chorus.

"Look, someone's in the pod—"

"It's Yamada."

"Come on, Yamada, what are you—"

"He's dead."

"What!"

More babble. "How did—" "What's he doing—" "By himself? Can't—" "Look, another pod's open." "Someone else, then?" "Come on, let's look."

I hear them searching behind the pods, through the showers, their voices rising and falling as they pass. I press

harder back, trying to blend into the wall and become featureless metal.

"No one here."

"Wait. What about behind there?"

I hold my breath.

"I'll check." Steps come closer, fast.

They stop by my hiding place. Something blocks the light
to the side. I can only stare, wide-eyed, not even able to
breathe, as Lopez's head pokes in, and his eyes peer into the
darkness. The light flicks on and its beam catches me full in
the face.

He looks. Straight at me. Straight through me.

And finally turns. "No one there," he says, and the beam is
gone.

"All right. Keep looking," I hear someone say. The babble
grows, becomes fainter, and then all is silent again after they
leave.

I ease out of the space and stand there, trembling. It is several minutes before I can think clearly.

Even then, I can't quite comprehend what has happened.
They heard us; they discovered Yamada dead. But they did
not see me. Lopez has no reason to cover up for me. To him I
actually did not exist.

I am grateful for that, to be sure. My apparent invisibility
barely saved me from Elimination. But underneath my gratitude, I feel uneasy about it, for it is still another strange circumstances I can't explain.

They must have some explanation—some end, some purpose. But what is it?

To those not part of our little group I am, in effect, invisible. But the others can still see me. They must be careful now
that no outsiders are around when they talk with me. That is,
if they talk with me at all.

"Hello, Macombray. What's new?" I slide into the chair
next to him at the rear table of the dining hall.

He is startled at my presence, then looks quickly to either

side. "What do you want?" he says, in an undertone full of malice.

"Why, just to make conversation," I say, spreading my hands. "Small talk. Passing some time. You know."

"Get away from me. You're poison now." He turns his back.

"Now that's not a nice thing to say," I say in an aggrieved tone. "You might hurt my feelings. Then who'll have duals with you?"

He turns back to me slowly. "You unspeakable monster. You killed Yamada in the dual session, and you expect us all to go on as if nothing happened? How can you be so inhuman?"

I shrug. "He had a weak mind. Too weak to take the risk or the consequences. I have no patience with anyone like that."

"This is a human life you're talking about," he says with barely controlled rage. "Don't you feel any guilt? Don't you have any feelings?"

"Why should I? He knew it was dangerous. We all do. He just wasn't equipped to handle it, that's all."

"You'll get caught. Don't worry about that."

"How?" I say, leaning forward. *"They* can't see me. *They* found no traces of anyone else in the dream-chamber. *They* didn't even find the settings changed. As far as *they* are concerned, I don't exist. Better this way, too. It'll make our arrangements easier."

"You actually expect us to go on?" Macombray looks at me with astonishment.

"Of course. You just do as I say, and everything will go smoothly."

"There will be no more duals." He spoke in a determined tone.

"That's what you say. Let's see how long you can stay away."

"No. No more," he repeats—but I can see the conflict on his face.

"Think about it," I say, and get up and leave.

Perhaps they do feel that way—afraid, scared off. But their need is greater. Though some will stay away, there are still others who will go on. Whether it is because of their need, or perhaps a thirst to strike a return blow, it doesn't matter, as long as they come back.

And later, when Fletcher accosts me in a darkened corridor, tight-lipped but assenting, I know I am right.

"You believed, didn't you?" I say. "You actually thought you could win this time. Oh, you had some good moments, that's true. But you proved wrong in the end. Do you realize that now?"

Fletcher can only moan. Her mouth gapes open, revealing the blackened cavity where her tongue used to be.

"What? I can't understand you, dear Fletcher." I edge the knife blade a little deeper, scoring along the edge of her rib cage. I thrust myself up into her rhythmically, hypnotically. Her body jerks and writhes, and her hands clench in the tightly knotted ropes above her head.

"I must keep this calm and methodical," I say to myself. "No fiery emotions. No fits of passion. Clinical and meticulous, that's what I must be."

Fletcher does not answer. I continue.

But when I wake, I find it has happened again, and Fletcher's corpse is sprawled half out of the coffin. I can only dress hurriedly and flee.

Running. Hiding. They all search for me now, all those I once dominated. I have avoided them up to now, but who knows how close they are on my heels? Two deaths— awakened their sense of decency, it seems. They will have no more of me.

Decency? In them? I could laugh.

But not now. No time for that. Only for reprisal and what they call justice.

There—the dream-room. —No. First place they'd look. Someplace else, but where?

"There he is. Get him!" Footsteps coming quickly.

I dodge around the corridor as Sedjayev appears at the other end. "Come on, he's getting away." But I don't see them as I run wildly to the staircases, then duck inside and slam the security locks tight behind me.

I hear their muffled blows on the other side of the door. "Open up, Yang." "Try it." "No good." "To the records. Get the correct sequence. Hurry!" I hear their voices, too, but I don't answer. I'm too busy throwing back the safety hatches; once those are open, I climb through, and begin descending toward the inner core of the Ship.

The stairs stop at the catwalks, and I walk among the humming machines again. I feel more secure here—doors and hatches locked behind me, none of the technicians able to see me, except for that damnable Hotaling. But it's not her shift now. Safe, yes. Safer than if I locked myself in my—

Room? Where *is* my room? I can't remember the number. I can't even remember what it looks like.

Again this uncertainty. What is this? Why can't I remember?

Calmly now. Take my name: Yang, first name—what?

Occupation—what?

Pre-Ship life—what?

I feel panic now, and sudden sweat on my forehead and under my arms. My hands tremble almost uncontrollably, and I want to scream. Steady. Easy now. I force the fear down, with great effort. At last the trembling stops, and I breathe more easily, leaning on the catwalk rail for support.

I try to think clearly. Facts. I need some to hold on to, to prove my own existence to myself. Ship name? *Voyager I.* Remember that. Launchtime—unknown. Try another. Duration time? I check my chronometer. Between forty and fifty— forty-seven. Yes. Forty-seven periods Ship-time. I have that, at least. That must be how long since launch-time, then. Converting back into earth years, that's—

The sound of slamming metal, and I start at the sudden beam of light down the catwalk. "Yes, I heard him going down here—" One voice comes, out of a loud babble. They have found me again.

I turn and run. The narrow catwalk curves and swoops around the great metal bulks; my fleeing footsteps ring in the cavernous engine chambers, along with their pursuit. I glance back at every turn, wasting a precious fraction of a second each time. They are gaining on me.

Damn them and their conspiracy! I can only think that as I whip past branching corridors, their lighting blinking on my dark path like beacons. I don't know where I'm going—or do I? I haven't been here before, I'm sure, but I am heading somewhere definite. Where, I don't know; I don't think about that—only about getting away.

There. That corridor. Down four doors, left at the next branch. I hear them still behind me. Four more doors, through the double palmprint-activated hatches—then unlocking the four complicated locks on the door with the title NO ADMITTANCE OF UNAUTHORIZED PERSONNEL UNDER ANY CIRCUMSTANCES.

Never mind that. The locks spring open at my bidding, almost magically. As the door whirs open, they appear at the end of the corridor. "There! He's going in!" "Stop him!" they shout as they rush forward.

But they are too slow. Quickly I am inside, and the door booms shut on them, and I reset the locks from the inside. Sudden exhaustion overcomes me, and I have to lean against the door; I feel their ineffectual poundings as slight tremors through the thick metal. It goes on and on, but it doesn't matter. They can't get in. I am safe.

Exhaustion gives way to elation, and I begin to laugh, shortwinded as I am. "Fools," I shout. "Go ahead. Keep pounding. You'll never get in." Still laughing, I turn—and the laughter dies away, as I see where I am.

The room is high, not wide, and softly lit. Against the walls on either side are enclosed rows of tanks, the glassteel banded by protecting metal. Within are solutions, bubbled through with gas feed lines. Floating in them are gray shapeless lumps, each with many wire leads going back and away: the Stables.

I've done it. I've found the Stables' chambers—the room of our rulers. The room of my—

My—

Something strange, rising in me. It reaches my throat, becoming a moan, then a groan, and then I am screaming, over and over again. I claw at the door, scratching to get out, to get away from them, those horrible gray lumps, throwing the relays, spinning the locks wildly until I hit the right combination and the door slides open and I tumble out into the midst of the others, who instinctively back away.

I get to my feet. "Stay back," I say. My voice quavers uncontrollably. "Don't come near me."

They circle around me, wary, ever watchful. They look at me with—fear? No. A wide-eyed horror and fascination. And something akin to—pity.

"Poor little phantom." I can hear it in Macombray's voice.

"What do you mean by that?" I demand. "What are you going to do?"

"Nothing. Nothing at all." Macombray points at me. "Do you know who you are? What you are?"

"What is this? I'm Yang. A crew member, like you."

"Are you? What happened in there?" He points to the chamber behind me. I fight a horrifying urge to look back.

"Nothing. A queasiness. Don't come closer." I back up against the door for support.

"Don't you think we heard the screams?" Ostermeyer says. "Would the sight of the Stables be that horrible to a crew member? Or did you react like that because you couldn't face yourself?"

"What kind of idiocy is this?" I say. "I'm as much a crew member as the rest of you. I came on board forty-seven periods ago, just like you did—"

"Forty-seven?" Ostermeyer turns to Lee. "Tell him."

Lee says, "I checked records for the hatch locks. I also called for the roster. There is no Yang on it."

"No," I say. "Impossible."

"And Ship launch was fifty earth-years ago, real time. On this Ship, the equivalent of seventy-eight periods."

"Liar," I say angrily, and swing at Lee. But my hand—my arm—they pass right through him. He stands there, untouched.

"That's right," he says, smiling sadly. "We know you now. And because we do, you become less effective. And less real."

I feel confusion and terror like a whirlpool around me. "But then—what—"

Macombray points behind me once more. "Look again," he says. "Face yourself this time."

And turn. I do not want to look, but I turn anyway. Against my will, I look again into the shadowy chamber, and see myself—

I am a great gray shapeless thing, grown *in vitro* from tissue cultures, kept in a saline nutrient solution maintained at thirty-seven degrees plus or minus point two degrees Centigrade, sustained by external voltage of seven plus or minus point one millivolts and by oxygen bubbler kept constant at thirty dynes per square centimeter pressure. I am used as guidance, intellect, psychologist/psychiatrist, and for data-storage, computation, Ship maintenance, and all cognitive functions. I am responsibile for maintenance of the internal, adiabatic world of the Ship on its years-long journey to other stars. Responsible for well-being of crew members, keeping them as close to psychological and social norms as possible, and eliminating all aberrant factors. In short, a Stable.

No.

"A figment of a Stable's imagination. Maybe too much oxygen pressure, or a fluctuation in solution pH. No matter. We've located the defective Stable. We should have known it before, with your access to 'confidential' files, and how easily you were able to readjust the machines . . ." Lee shakes his head.

"But what now?" I plead. I can only plead, now.

"We deactivate you. After a while."

"What do you mean?" I say with apprehension. They all look at me. Accusers.

"You treated us like things," Lee says. "You took advantage of us—of our weaknesses—playing with them and toying with us for your own perverted games. But you're only a phantom. We, on the other hand, are human. We *feel*. When you took us into dream, we felt all the pain and terror and agony you wanted us to feel. After all that, we could hate, and ache for revenge.

"That's what we're going to do now: take a little revenge. And we have you to thank for showing us the way." They all turn and begin to leave.

"Wait," I say, reaching for them. "What do you intend to do?"

Lee turns. He is smiling. "We're going to have a little dream," he says. "But don't feel left out. You'll be in it."

"No," I say. "No. No!"

But it's no use. I can't stop them. All I can do is wait, huddled with fear, until they come for me, and take me, and—

Strap me to the table, split my belly open with knives, and pull the organs out—

Whittle my limbs slowly down to stubs with glittering blades—

Tear my skin off with snapping bullwhips—

Shoot me—

Brain me—

Castrate me—

Disembowel me—

Again and again. A hundred times, a thousand, until I beg for it to end, for them to stop.

But it doesn't stop. Oblivion doesn't come.

They lied. They're going to torture me forever. As I used them, so they're now using me. And I can do nothing except die, over and over again.

They've learned well.

As our technology continues to grow and proliferate, permeating every corner of our society, it opens new possibilities for everyone: new careers, new abilities . . . and new crimes. It may soon be possible (if it isn't already) for an industrial spy with the key information to steal every bit of computerized data a company has stored—and he could do it with the same ease with which he might tap a phone. Then there are the other capabilities that go along with such technological crime. . . .

CHARLIE HAAS *was born in Brooklyn in 1952, studied writing at the University of California, Santa Cruz, and has sold stories to the men's slicks. At last report he was working on a historical novel.*

Shifting Parameters in Disappearance and Memory

BY CHARLIE HAAS

ONE

"A big change came into my life at that point, because I was suddenly *deluged* with information—information about life in general."

—JIMMY WEBB, songwriter,
interviewed in *The New Yorker,* January 9, 1971

The second call had me expecting something out of an espionage movie: At 2:13 in the same diner as last time you'll get directions to a noisy bar in an Asian port where the fat man with the ginger-colored beard and the eyepatch will hand you a tan briefcase, electronically sealed, containing five forged telegrams, a yellow capsule, a thermos of vodka martinis.

Work on your silence. Anyone who needs you can spot the rolling, aikido-tempered walk, the all-but-obsolete precision tailoring, the apparent vague distaste around the nose and mouth—a grimace, actually, of jet-lag and near-deaths catching up with you, drying remote tissues. They're watching and they're fast, how fast we can't say, but this is how it always is, passing overnight from each smoky city to the next without a trace.

But the third call dispelled that, and I didn't think that way again for a few weeks. The phone rang twice before I got to it but only because I stood up and walked around the counter when I could have reached. I was in the breakfast nook, a half-room with dimmer-switch lighting, where high-backed wrought-iron chairs with thin round avocado-colored cushions on their seats and backs surrounded a short white counter. The catalog had listed the cushions in avocado, bone, brandywine, and flamenco. The chairs came high-backed or low-backed, and with the cushions you could go for your circle or your soft-cornered square. By nature I am a friend to catalogs. But I am an enemy of multiplicities generated solely to fake freedom of choice, a runoff of pointless options in which the colors take code names and seek cover in print. The carpet was sherry, which was red. The house, my house, was in Beverly Hills, and the tan telephone, one of those new rectangular instruments with the dial on the underside of the receiver, looked like an iced maple bar from Mr. Donut. I had two such maple bars cued up on a plate on the counter; that's how I noticed. The plate was Malibu, blood-red with a double black racing stripe. The stripes were parallel chords of varied thickness, which extended the plate's area, while the concentric version, also available, confined it.

"Hello?" I said.

"This shouldn't be difficult." A young male voice, long distance.

"Should I get a pencil?"

"You know Sacramento airport?"

"No," I said.

"Can you fly up tonight?"

"Which flight?"

"Anything that gets in early, like before ten."

"Who are you?" I said.

"Steve Golden will come out and pick you up. He should be there about then, about ten, but if he doesn't show up after a while you could call him. You just wait in the coffee shop."

"What's his number?"

"It would be in the phone book. It's on S Street. That's where you're going. Or you could call information, it might be new."

"Okay."

"Only it might not be under his name. Oh no, yeah it would, yeah. For sure."

"And he plans to get me at ten?"

"Well, he might be doing something first, but he'll get over there if his car is okay. You should use a different name when you buy the ticket. You need anything?"

I picked up a maple bar. "I don't think so," I said. He hung up. That was the third call, the last one. The second call, which had set me up for intrigue, came about half an hour earlier in the same room.

"We really like what you did," the girl said when I answered the phone.

"You said that before," I said. "Who is this?"

"Have you figured out what to do next?"

"No," I said, holding the receiver with my shoulder, picking up a Ho Ho and unwrapping it. This was before I found the maple bars in a bag in the breadbox.

"We can get you out of there," the girl said.

"Who are you?"

"You want to get out for a few weeks?"

I was licking the icing on the Ho Ho and holding it too tightly. Flakes of chocolate fell on the counter. "To where?" I said.

"We'll just put you up in this house with some people up here and you can just stay there for a few weeks, okay?"

"How?"

"We'll call you back," she said, and hung up. I finished the
Ho Ho in four bites, then made the fallen flakes stick to my
thumb and licked them off.

The first call came about twenty minutes before that, upstairs. The same girl said they liked what I had done and then
hung up right away. I went downstairs to get something to
eat.

I put the second maple bar back in its bag and put the bag
in one of the side pockets of my carry-on suitcase. After I
finished packing I drove out to the swimming club where my
wife, Elaine, was swimming with my children, Aaron and
Kimberly, and left a note under the windshield wiper of her
car.

In May 1968, in Los Angeles, you could subject your skin
and throat to the air for hours and get no reading at all: it was
still more like remembering heat than being in it. The reason
you feel so unsupported, so singled out, by the spring and
summer weather there is that the brightness and dryness have
taken all the *presence* out of the air and what you wind up
with is essentially static, stubbing your lungs on each thin
sample.

I put the car in long-term parking and made a six-thirty
flight, reading the L.A. *Times* late edition and eating
Zaanland chocolate from the gift shop all the way to
Sacramento. There was nothing about me in the *Times* that
day, but it took me a long time to get through it because I was
blocking, which I do sometimes. I see a headline, such as
PARK BOARD ASKS $ TWO MILLION, and my concentration is
too scattered to register it, so without thinking about it I find
myself abstracting it further and silently hearing some varia-
tion like *They want the two million,* or *The parks are asking
for the dollars now, great,* or even *Where am I going to get
two million dollars?,* all part of an intensive involuntary program aimed at the sense. Meanwhile there's the guilty sensa-
tion of trying to repair something by forcing it, the one

method you're never supposed to use. It does make the newspaper last longer, and I love the paper as much as anyone, so
maybe that's the cause. Except that I don't apply it to just the
newspaper, but to my situation as well. At least once a day
the surroundings and circumstances blank, like a word spoken
several times so that first its meaning goes and then even its
existence is implausible. Apart from the immediate problems,
this is exactly what was responsible for my taking the nearly
empty jet to Sacramento in the first place. I'm neither slow
nor stupid and I mean to understand, but in numerous cases
the interference has been prohibitive. And it's not just me, it's
everybody, restating most of what comes in and waiting for
something to click.

In Sacramento I bought a *Time* at the airport newsstand
and took it to the coffee shop, where I ordered a roast beef
sandwich, cole slaw, cherry pie, and coffee. I couldn't start
eating or reading for a few minutes after I got the food,
though, because a string arrangement of "Wichita Lineman"
started on the airport Muzak and I had to listen to it.

This was right in the middle of the period when Jimmy—
Jimmy L. Webb, the Los Angeles songwriter—had so many
songs being played on the radio at once. I don't imagine that I
was hearing them unusually often, since they were hits, but
the frequency of chance encounter was working out to about
once every two days, what with the Glen Campbell and Fifth
Dimension things catching on almost simultaneously, and
then Richard Harris right on top of that with his all-Jimmy
album. In Los Angeles you're dealing with a radio economy,
which is to say that radio is assumed into the atmosphere as a
commonly negotiable presence independent of its own content. In no other city do you undergo as many air minutes a
day, invited through your own receiver or enforced by others,
nor can you hear station preferences defended as heatedly by
as many laymen. In big places there is always the need for private entertainment along with the fear of missing something,
but the biggest consideration where these station loyalties are

concerned is format. Not just format in the sense of voice preference and jingle preference, which do exist, but in the sense that some programming practices involve more listener risk than others. Meaning: in its simultaneity of production and consumption, radio has the means of abrogating your right to screen by bringing to your attention what you'd rather let go. Sometimes format knows best, and sometimes the most pressing matters will find their own channels. In my own case, for example, I wasn't much concerned with music and not at all with the music industry, but the Jimmy Webb songs became important immediately, the first time I heard "By the Time I Get to Phoenix." I was in the middle of changing stations in the car, Glen was in the middle of the second stanza, my hand dropped, and my voluntary and involuntary facilities chose up sides then and there and have never really reconciled since. Immediately I heard myself thinking: What am I doing listening to *this*, to this gummy, gleaming International Harvester of a song, with some moping hayseed counting off the names of bus-station cities, shipping out from one to the next?

But at the same moment my heart locked on that sound and it was literally all I could do to remember that I was driving. Not only was I transfixed, not only did I sense correctly that I was committing the song and Glen's arrangement to permanent memory on first hearing, but I could feel some awful jamming applied to my veins, glands, and organs, a battery of interior gushes and starts such as I'd never before had and no music should have produced. My eyes lost focus, and while I could concentrate on the song enough to know that I shouldn't have liked it, I was unable to think of anything else until it was over and my tissues, liquid and solid, had been shunted back into place inside. The overriding impression, even then, was that I had been listening to something I wasn't supposed to have heard, that a serious mistake had been made. When the same thing happened with "MacArthur Park," "Up, Up, and Away," and the others, I started an active file of the titles on a Wil Wright's bag and had soon isolated the composer as the unifying factor. I had no informa-

tion on him beyond that when I arrived in Sacramento. I'd
been doing nothing about my reaction to the songs, just waiting it out, even though I'm fat so these physical things scare
me and "Up, Up, and Away" had been picked up and adapted
as an airline commercial, pushing the incidence up a little.

So I was understandably interested to see, when the song
was over, that there was an article about Jimmy in the *Time*
I'd bought, called "Up, Up, & Away in 18 Months." Raised in
Oklahoma and Texas, Beatle-coifed tunesmith Webb, twenty-
one, had studied music at San Bernardino Valley College but
dropped out because of his mother's death and because he
was—quoting the article—"struggling to sort out his life."
Then he broke up with this girl he'd met at San Bernardino
Valley and wrote "By the Time I Get to Phoenix," his first hit,
about the experience. Smashes became a matter of habit for
the youthful cleffer, and now his twenty-two-room house in
Hollywood was—quoting again here—

a raucous rehearsal hall for clients and colleagues. Self-
possessed amid the noise and confusion, he still manages to get
to his Yamaha concert grand or his electric organ to work on
new music, sometimes with incredible facility (he wrote "Up,
Up, and Away" in 35 minutes).

Everything written about Jimmy during that period calls attention to this thirty-five-minute business, and I've made a
point of seeing all the literature on him. The piece in *Time*
also quoted some lyrics from "MacArthur Park," which was
just starting to make new friends for the heartbroken fireball
then ("MacArthur Park is melting in the dark,/All the sweet
green icing flowing down . . ."), and said that these were
"typical of his personal and provocative imagery."

Then, in the Business section, there was an article about
me, "Vacco and TTW: On the Blink," saying I had

simply stopped coming to work early last month, leaving senior
staffers at TechTron West no choice but to declare his snug
$30,000 annual berth as Executive Vice-President temporarily
—but alarmingly—open.

Phone calls to Vacco's Beverly Hills home only deepened the
mystery, according to Creative Head Marvin Loewinson, who

shares credit with the absentee VP—a balding, taciturn, 46-
year-old former Wesleyan physics professor—for shaping TTW
into a "little giant" in the systems implementation area.

"We'd call him up," Vacco's colleague told a *Time* reporter,
"and as soon as he heard it was one of us on the phone—
[Chairman Lewis] Brophy and I were calling a few times a
week—he'd start playing these crazy tape recordings into the
phone, just weird sound assemblages, pieces of old radio
dramas and news broadcasts and whatnot. He's got quite a library of tapes out there, so I guess he's been spending a lot of
time splicing them together and so on, I don't know." Visits to
Vacco's house proved no less frustrating, with Vacco greeting
guests cordially, then refusing to discuss any subject but the Los
Angeles Dodgers' pennant prospects in the current season.
"That's the other strange thing," Loewinson mused at week's
end, "Justin was never what you'd call a big baseball fan. I
don't even look to them as contenders myself."

Pieces into place

Indeed, if Vacco had leisure interests, he kept them to himself
during his seven-year tenure at TTW, maintaining a low personal profile and garnering a reputation for fair but firm
decision-making in a field characterized by fast shifting of costs
and prices against a free-swinging competitive backdrop.

Vacco's colleagues at TTW and elsewhere in the mini-
mushrooming industry were ready to write off his actions as an
aberration of personal behavior, until an investigatory audit last
week revealed that over $600,000 in corporate funds had been
"abstracted"—Chairman Brophy's euphemism for the complex
and as-yet still-to-be-unraveled financial gymnastics which allowed the money's disappearance to go unnoticed for so long,
and its actual whereabouts to remain a stern cipher at press
time. Vacco's antics are being watched more seriously now, and
TTW lawyers have advised him that a full investigation,
spearheaded by the firm in cooperation with IRS, SEC, and
U. S. Attorney's Office personnel, begins next week.

"Once you see the disappearance of the funds," Loewinson
observed darkly, "pieces start falling into place."

Well, okay. Actually there's misinformation there, and I'm
not concerned as much about the kind you can pinpoint and

refute on a factual basis as I am about the over-all miscarriage of meaning. The people who write news put a lot of emphasis on accuracy in regard to specifics, which diverts attention from their real problem. If you talk to the individuals whose moves have been the subject of any reporting that is in the least interpretive, or who were present at reported events, their final assessment is almost always the same: even when the details are right, even in accounts by participants, the feeling at the event and the feeling given off by the record don't match up. The reporter's empathy and understanding may be perfect, but the essence's resistance to being caught is better than perfect, is magnetic, is beyond his control, and so reliably it will steal a nuance and ruin him. The honest reporter knows he can't be honest.

Not that specific incorrect statements are any help. I played one of my tapes over the phone only once, when Lewis Brophy called up, and at that point I was still frightened. It was only a week after I'd stopped coming to work. I handled the other phone calls pretty well, I thought, showing interest in office social life, asking smart production questions. They seemed like fairly pleasant phone calls to me; at least *I* made an effort to be pleasant. So that's where I started getting uncomfortable about the article, and then this thing about the Dodgers. The only time I brought up the Dodgers was when Marv Loewinson came out one evening in the third week, and then only because he was too embarrassed to carry on a normal conversation and I know *he* likes baseball. The other thing is that even then I wasn't "balding," but bald. I had no hair on my head. That's it. Bald. Bingo. But as I say, what frightens me most is the estrangement from the real feeling, and that's harder to track. Take this first thing, "simply stopped coming to work." In the computer industry, nobody simply stops, even if they think they have. How could they? Once you're using a programmed symbolic language like that you don't just turn your back on it and go quiet when you want out. You *owe* that system something. Think of what it's done for you, for all the people who worked where I did: it gave them the privilege, the opportunity, to get their hands on signals, frequencies, vibrations, the same stuff that's within them, an opportunity to increase rarity and preciousness. Predictably, they refused to recognize that, insisting instead on acting as if it were all numbers. This way they get to have *mature responses*, something they always wanted. You can tell they were once quiet kids who tinkered, because some of them are still a little creepy, but in any case there's very little that's beyond their capacity to accept and account for. If something is beyond them, they're pretty calm about that too, because it's not in their area and nobody's going to bother them about it. Meanwhile their areas are shrinking. But what good is an expert's knowledge without an expert's attitude? Knowing the implications of what you're doing makes all the difference in the world. What you owe the system, when you're ready to go, is the respect indicated by your expertise, the comprehension needed to invade all areas simultaneously and plot the reaction. So I sat it out until I was good enough, reading sales reports and newspaper headlines every day and seeing the meanings squirm and tease like code. When the code broke was when I went to Sacramento. The last bits of information I looked up were two names in the phone book, a first one and a last one. I used them to get out.

But remember what a factor interference is, for the *Time* people as well as for me. Later that year, around Christmas, *Newsweek* did a piece on Jimmy, called "Webb of Music." It mentioned that he had "developed expensive tastes in clothes, his wardrobe running from a $1,000 spotted silver sealskin coat to Italian hiphuggers and brown pigskin bell-bottomed pants." But what you want to watch are the contradictions with the *Time* article. The lost girl friend who touched off "By the Time I Get to Phoenix" was now the drill-team captain at Jimmy's high school instead of a college classmate, and the reason for quitting college in this version was that his "music professor said, 'Why don't you do yourself and the college a favor and try to become a songwriter in LA.'" *Newsweek* also said "MacArthur Park" was "overblown," which moves the contradictions to the critical level.

So it's not hard to see how these things get scrambled, and in one sense it's all for the best. One condition under which Jimmy operates is that his material be strongly sentimental, and he's in contact with it all the time; it gets all over him. So hopefully he can contain several legends. I was in the business of permutations, and wanted no less for myself. Already there were two versions, mine and theirs. Let's take that into account. Because we're going at an elegant problem here. We can start thinking of these discrepancies as *increments of romance*. Does that help?

I sat there, in my Navy chinos, white polo shirt and white canvas deck shoes, eating my white salad in the fogbound airport and waiting for my ride. First I worried about whether he'd show up and then about whether he'd be a safe driver, because I'm frightened of accidents. But as it turned out the kid had a convincing style. I asked him if he'd been listening to jazz and he said yes. He had a jazz system, immediately distinguishable from rock driving, which is what you see so much of in LA. The rock driver, trusted with a standard shift, automatically regards the top end of each gear as a climactic dominant chord preceding a break and leans on it for several bars of crescendo before he upshifts. With Steve Golden there were no such cheap releases, but an extended flexibility of speed and steering that dealt with each dark street on its own terms. I got comfortable and then I got sleepy. In half an hour we were there, a two-story white frame house on S Street. He led me up the stairs to a room with a cot. There was also a desk, but no chair, and a small table lamp with a red lampshade on the floor beside the bed. I went right to sleep.

The airport was separate from town, the distance supported by flat farm fields. I counted four dead animals on the road, a dog and three cats or raccoons. The fog broke as soon as we got away from the airport. Steve said the airport was in the foggiest part of the valley, that if there was fog anywhere in

Sacramento on a given day, there would be fog at the airport. He told me the house we were going to had four people living in it: himself, one other man, and two women. He said all four were working on artistic and political projects. His was devising a new reading program for illiterate adults. He said his household and their friends had decided to get me out of LA before the investigation started, if I wanted to go, because they liked what they'd read about me, particularly the part about playing the tapes over the phone. The wire services had played that up. He laughed about it when he mentioned it and turned to look at me. I smiled.

He found me in the coffee shop at ten-thirty, just as I was about to go and call him. He was very tall and thin, wearing a dark green T-shirt, blue jeans, and black basketball sneakers. His red hair was short and curly. He was twenty-two or twenty-three. I immediately noticed how pleasant he was being, and he in turn noticed that I was relieved. I picked up my suitcase, the *Time*, and the *Times*, and we went out to the car, a copper-colored Mustang, a few years old, and then he drove me to the house on S Street where I was going to stay with him and his friends. I slept there, all night.

TWO

"I know I need a small vacation
But it don't look like rain."
—JIMMY WEBB, "Wichita Lineman"

The door to my room opened and a boy walked in and started taking photographs of me with a 35-millimeter camera. A Pentax. He didn't knock first, or try to be quiet so I wouldn't wake up; he just walked in, went into a professional squat, and started snapping. He moved the camera away from his face between shots so he could size up angles without using the view-finder while he advanced the film with the little thumb-lever. His expression was the anxious look of someone concentrating on detail work, pulling his eyebrows close together and his lower lip between his teeth. He had big eyes, al-most round, a short thin mouth and straight blond hair combed back. He was wearing a dark blue shirt and a white necktie, cuffed cream trousers and hiking shoes. He took eight or nine pictures of me opening my eyes, sitting up a little, squinting, lying down again, and turning my face to the pillow. His exposure was half a second, littering the room with short buzzes. I kept hearing them after he took his last picture and left.

I was staring, trying to think of something to say. He was assigning so much analysis work to his eyes that he never focused on my face, so it was hard to get his attention even though he was watching me.

I got dressed and went downstairs. The hallway was narrow and freshly painted light blue. Opposite my door were the stairs. Downstairs, on the open left side, was a yellow living room containing a sofa with an Indian bedspread on it, a brown armchair, a table covered with books and newspapers, the radio, the phonograph, and two old floor lamps with beige shades. To the right of the stairs was a wall with a doorway in it, and straight ahead was the front door. The floors were clean, bare wood, and there was a lot of natural light.

Through the doorway on the right, at the foot of the stairs, was a square orange kitchen. The boy with the camera sat fac-ing the door at a low wooden table, drinking tea. To his right was a dark pretty girl in pigtails whose breasts jiggled in her Mexican blouse as she reached for the teapot to refill her cup.

I walked in and stood at the other end of the table, near the door. She looked up at me.

"Hi," she said, smiling. "I'm Pat."

"I'm Justin," I said. The boy looked into his teacup. "You may remember taking my photograph a little earlier."

He looked up, watched me for a few seconds, then turned and spoke to the girl. "You know what you want to do when you go into a room like that to shoot?" he asked her. "You get parallel to one wall and then pick out two or three basic angles." Holding his hands flat and overlapping the thumbs, he made a rectangle with a missing side and began framing portions of the air around him. His fingers swelled slightly at the tips, forcing little cracks between them when he held them together. Light from the window behind him fell through the cracks and hit the table in long stripes, dimmed and spread a little by the distance.

He looked at me again. "Now as a physicist," he said, "you see what you're going up against with still photography. The limitations." He waved distractedly at the camera in front of him on the table. "I wanted to get something on your face right away, though."

"You want some tea?" Pat asked.

"Where's Steve?" I said.

"He's at the reading project," Pat said.

The boy turned toward the shelf behind him, half standing, and brought down a blue enameled mug from the same set they were using. "The question is," he said, pouring, "how fast we can go from stills to film."

"Film of me?"

He nodded. "Would you have just stayed in LA for the investigation?" he asked.

"What's your name?" I said.

"Michael. You would have been guilty, right?" As he pushed the cup toward me, a floating layer of brown residue sifted to the bottom, first long diamond-shaped flakes, then threads, and finally the loose powder. "So you couldn't stay there."

"I guess not," I said.

Pat saw me staring at the tea. "It's herbal," she said. It had a raw sweet flavor and no smell. I didn't want to swallow the leaves. I put my upper teeth against the edge of the cup to act as a screen.

"What bothers me is this, though," Michael said. "You had to go into a lot of different computers to get the money out, right? So there's an access problem."

"Why computers?" Pat asked.

"There was no way to get at the accounts for so much money except by diverting it in the computers," Michael said. "So let's say you wrote all your programs in advance to make the changes in the accounts." My cup was half full. He refilled it and leaned closer to me. "But it's not just your computer," he continued, "that's the problem. There's the bank, the accounting company, figure a couple of brokers. So how do you get in?" Over his shoulder, on the wall beside the window, above the stove, was a black-and-white mounted photograph with no border. It was of an overturned highway-patrol car with broken windows, taken on a city street at night with a lot of people running in the background.

"You don't have to worry about swallowing any of the leaves and stuff," Pat said. "It's just herbs." Michael made a shutter adjustment and took a shot of me putting down my teacup.

"But most of those computers have the phone terminals now, for receiving from other units," Michael was saying. "And they record the entries, which is another problem. But what if you put together some sort of independent equipment of your own that got you in past the defenses by imitating the authorized signal? Then you could put your program through. It's all audio frequencies, just like long distance. So with the right whistles you can go right through. What we should do now is to get as much footage together as possible before you have to leave the country and I have to go to Chicago."

"Leave the country?" I said.

"Michael got a grant to shoot the Democratic convention," Pat said. "I'm doing car pools for it."

"Which gives us about a month to shoot here," Michael said.

"To shoot what?" I asked.

"Yours is our main story. Your theft, or the technology of the theft, which is going to be very important soon. And I fold that in with my convention stuff after I edit—"

"I can't be in any movie," I said.

"Why not?" Pat said.

"Because I'm hiding."

"Ah," said Michael. "That's where you need me."

"Why?" I said.

"Because you can hide things in film that you can't hide in stills. Film pictures don't stay around to be investigated. Once you get in there you can disappear, right? It's like: how often do you get to say 'Life has been passing me by' and make it stick? Does that make sense?"

"No," I said.

"Okay," he said without stopping, "try this. Nobody gets to hide anymore. Physically. I mean, if it was you they wanted they'd have you; we weren't that sneaky about getting you up here in the first place."

"Was that you on the phone?" I said.

"Only it's not you they're looking for. They're looking for your signal, which at this point is in and out of circuits like nothing." He moved his head as if watching something very fast. "Hundredth of a second, bang. And they can't get it to stand still. It's like a moving picture. So you're already hidden. Now if you want to *stay* hidden, you have to keep putting out code. Up there." He put his hand out, between the window and the wall, then pulled it in toward himself, so that the shadow was sharp, then blurry, then gone. "On the screen."

"All I did was leave my job," I said absently.

"Yeah, but why?" he said.

"Because I couldn't concentrate." I was watching Pat. Her breasts knocked together as she spread some apple butter on a piece of bread; then they wiggled back to stillness. But forget the breasts, just look at the action itself, the decaying harmonic motion. Pick a nipple, or a pore or something, and it's doing it, under the sheer white cloth of the blouse. This is the charm that pulls you into physics to begin with: things know what to do, all by themselves. In this case they were dividing the motion into smaller and smaller percentages of the original, so that someone can plot it and it's perfectly regular, but that's later, after the fact. When I was fifteen I was reading a book in which the author said that some falling object, I forget what, "described an arc." I loved that, *"described,"* because the object was telling how the arc looked without saying anything. The pure action has no contents. Pat put down the knife and it started again.

"You think you could get that money now," Michael was saying, "or part of it?"

"What for?" I said.

"We'll need some equipment," he said, "and you'll have to make some more of your boxes if we're going to get the story down."

"You don't understand," I said. "I'm not even going to do this. I haven't even admitted doing what you're talking about."

He stood and picked up his camera. "That's the end of a roll," he said. "I have to go develop these. Let me make you some prints. I'll want to get some more on your face before we go into shooting," and then he was gone.

After all this happened, I started seeing literature on the so-called phone freaks, who had figured out that long-distance telephone calls are connected by computers and that the computers are cued into action by audio frequencies. The frequencies connected the home-phone line to the long-distance lines while the call was registered for billing. So by imitating those frequencies, either through human whistling or homemade electronic boxes, the freaks were able to bypass the equipment. Consequently their calls seemed to originate not at their own telephones but in the unpopulated distance between terminals, popping up in the middle somewhere and making only the second part of the trip. Free service, and then the compounded manipulation of frequencies and equipment, stacking connections and calling all the way around the world for nothing.

Still later, it became public knowledge that many business computers have telephone capabilities, set up so that a programmer could have access to the memory banks and

processing facilities, using his authorized equipment to identify himself by producing the right frequencies. Once he heard
the entry tone coming back at him, he was in, and could then
introduce or withdraw material by continuing to use his
equipment, which translated his instructions from programming language into frequencies, which the computer could re-
translate over the phone. Soon enterprising unauthorized individuals discovered that the tones and equipment could be
duplicated, and they were impersonating the password-
holders, plugging information in and out to alter memories.
Entire programs were being stolen. Every phone was a potential terminal for every computer, given a widespread knowledge of the technical basics.

None of this should have been surprising. Once you get
used to the idea of everything being made of frequencies, you
can circumvent nearly any defense, and the kind of people
who can make beeping boxes from hi-fi scraps have been used
to that idea for years.

But when you gain entry to one place, you leave another.
Given that you know what you're doing for what it is, you
finally find, without time to gear up, that now *you* are the signal, with no weight, no shape, an instantaneous lifespan, and
almost infinite speed! Studying the equipment for a long time
makes the difference. The basic working part, the place where
you spend most of your time on the inside, is a minuscule
chip covered with enough tiny hardware for one operation or
storage. You can always tell when you're in a memory, because the turns and straightaways are special. That's the wonderful thing about working with computers: that you can dis-
tinguish a memory from anything else.

Not that it's all smooth sailing out there in the nexus. There
are these terrible searing flashes that you recognize as floods
of electric impulses going through at the same time as you.
But in time you learn to recognize other things as well, and
when you look from overhead at a lighted city or a network of
rivers, or through a microscope at the compounding connections of nerves forming up into a brain, you make memory's

jaunty salute, snapping two fingers from your forehead at the first chill.

At any rate, what scared me then was that Michael should have figured out my operation in the summer of 1968, when I was the first, when there had been no publicity of any dimension. Other systems designers eventually unwound what I'd done, as I knew they would, but Michael was a layman who could think ahead, something I didn't need because I'd barely started formulating the practice of this aberrant wave of science and already someone was ready to apply and appropriate that practice on behalf of social theory. Einstein's dilemma, Nobel's, spending years of their lives trying to isolate stable solutions to contain their guilt, generating shock waves of embarrassing gestures, making things worse. I went into the living room and turned on the radio. In the summer of 1968, if you turned on the radio and waited, you would hear either news about political rioting of some kind or a song by Jimmy Webb. You almost couldn't listen for any length of time *without* hearing one or the other. In this case it was "Paper Cup," the follow-up to "Up, Up, and Away" by the Fifth Dimension.

Jimmy was hot and was using it on me. That whole week, living in that house in Sacramento, I knew every move he was making without being told because it was coming to me on the air. Jimmy alone, late at night, surrounded by soft light from the pool lamps as he tortures chords from the electric organ in the downstairs living room of the twenty-two-room house no more than five miles away from where my wife and children are sleeping. The drill team captain and the college classmate enter through opposite doors, peppy ghosts moving in mirror synch and talking with one voice, begging Jimmy to give it up and come upstairs. He closes his eyes. Later he gives them thirty-five minutes each. But right now he's writing. He hits a key, cocks an ear, and hums, stretching the pigskin along his thigh with a fast stab at a pedal. Jimmy has told a newsmagazine that he's worried about staying fresh, about not getting into a bag. Keeping those reporters away from the house is the best insurance, but he doesn't know that yet. It's wonderful to have incredible facility. He still does. He just checked. But now the pressure is on: nobody wants Jimmy to write an unsuccessful song. There are friends and colleagues everywhere now, and for their sake he has to sand his fingers before sitting down to play. But what's most remarkable is that one problem I have, living there in Sacramento that first week, is this intense lethargy, a much more serious problem than the intermittency of concentration I get in LA, and I begin to feel that Jimmy has gotten desperate and unscrupulous and is tapping *me*.

Remember that we live in a world arrayed by frequencies and that when we move, we are introducing more vibrations to a surrounding that already resonates. Everything conveyed within the body is by rates of vibration, and if someone who appreciates all this encodes a specific series of signals into a camouflage of music—well, now you have your first link. As long as those songs were on the radio, in the air, I was wide open, whether I listened or not. And when I did listen, the overload of directed energy was tangible.

People seem to think that a computer is a uniquely sterile and impervious domain, no noise in the programs, no dust, no static. What they forget is that every system has deposits forming at points of heat and motion. Similarly, there are those in every field who want to be experts, who will take the risk of touching the essential material, getting light or sound or some other vibration on their hands. Jimmy was aiming those songs at me, keying them to my entry frequencies, so that he could tap information—comparing notes, in effect, since we were really in the same field. Jimmy was a good working model of an expert because he understood what he was doing. The expert is one type of secret agent, a special case. Like the others, he goes where nobody knows him and where he remembers nothing, and he takes another name, or another form, even if it means becoming a physical outlaw, a refugee from the guidelines of matter and energy—whatever's necessary to eject himself to the place where he can get at the stuff. The findings are in on this one, fellas. *Le deluge, c'est moi.* And while the other agents have to take their capsules rather than tell you anything, we are meant to talk your ear off until we get back to where we started.

Standing there in that living room full of morning light as the song ended on the radio, I shuddered. I was thinking ahead. There's one frequency, and I've known this for as long as I can remember, this one frequency by which the cells of the body and the objects in the line of vision are held together. And that's the one you never hear because you're in it, you know that line of reasoning? And I became frightened, standing in that living room seven years ago, by the inexplicable certainty that there exists equipment for turning that frequency off, and that the equipment works.

I was sitting on the cot, eating the second maple bar, when Michael brought the prints up. Being unmounted left them open to stiff buckles and ripples across the surface of the paper. None of the images took all of its sheet. They sat at odd angles, their edges passing into watery white borders with only intermediary blurs. He was doing something wrong in the baths. You could see it best in those blank margins, where the set of the emulsion on the paper was most clearly visible, the chemicals' arrested sliding leaving rings like trapped cells. The sheets felt gummy.

In the first two pictures I turned my head from the pillow toward the door, squinting. In the third one I lifted my head and brought it forward.

I was holding them. Michael stood at my side, his hands hovering. He brought a finger down on the edge of the third print before I could flip past it.

"You see what you're doing here?" he said.

"Did you want this much contrast?" I said.

"See the way you're *bring*ing your head up?" He jerked his own head up fast, on the diagonal. "See how it pulls your eyes open really wide?" I looked at my eyes in the photograph: they were frightened, and trying to get me to look into them. I closed my eyes. "Okay, these next two," Michael went on, pulling away the third print and pushing it to the back of the stack, holding the fourth one above the fifth so I could see them both at once. I opened my eyes and looked. "Dropping the head halfway and then coming up again," he said. "See what you're doing with your neck here? I'm going to want that."

"Let's forget about the movie thing, okay?" I said. "I'm really tired." I tried to hand the prints back to him.

"You can keep this set," he said. "I did two. Look, why don't you come downstairs and we'll screen some pictures?" He was talking to my face in the fifth print, which was at the top of the stack. The eyes were closed.

Trying to assemble a consensus on Michael's movies, I've relied on available literature: film journals, radical magazines, no very popular reviewers because Michael has never had that wide an audience. I would have tried to do it all myself, but my critical language is far from adequate. And even though I own prints of all the films and have seen most of them fifteen or twenty times, I find that long sections of each one refuse to come to mind in any recognizable form unless they're on the screen in front of me. Somehow they resist not only memorization but simple recollection. At any rate:

In the early pictures (everything before *Cloud Chamber*), Michael establishes his comfort with conventional rhythmic cutting and planned sequence, at least on a shot-by-shot basis. Only in a larger framework—that of plot and continuity—is the interference felt. In *Governments* (1966), Ellen (Cathy Lewin) tells the hitchhiker (Bobby Roy, who later turns up in *Cloud Chamber* as the guidance counselor) a story about her having to leave a house just as a shipment of drugs is about to arrive there. Then, during what we would take to be the next morning (the hitchhiker, who's been sleeping on Ellen's couch, goes out; Ellen dresses and leaves immediately afterward), the episode she's described as a memory takes place in the present. No suggestion is made that this is a flashback or that she remembers either the incident or having talked about it. From the use of an omniscient viewpoint to trap her within the action, it's unmistakable that the event she's described and the one taking place are identical.

Claire Clouzot wrote a long piece about *Governments* for *Film Quarterly,* calling Ellen a direct representative of Michael's authority and "a fully realized person in the director's terms because she creates her experience by anticipating it," the first step toward creating in the films "a disruption of sequential time only insofar as a simultaneity, and thus an equality, are imparted to all memories and events."

But in *Cloud Chamber* (1967), a single action—the guidance counselor takes the list of drug-users' names from Celia (Sue Rice, who is Tinda in *Apparatus of the Carnival* [1969] —is staged and filmed four different ways. Lines are exchanged and visual relationships reversed; the office space contracts and expands as Michael changes point-of-view and angle coverage from one rendition to the next. Sympathy, malevolence, detachment, and cordiality are permuted. Increasingly, everything takes too much or too little time to happen, and sequence is abandoned. Philip T. Hartung, questioning this method, says the "literal accumulation of alternatives fabricates a contrived uncertainty, a forced deprivation of judgments."

In a series of five scenes at the end, Celia decides to leave town after the third confrontation between the students and the construction crew working in the vacant lot across the street from the school. These last scenes, taking about twenty minutes, are silent (the student ringleader, Fred Spiegel, asks Celia earlier: "How would you like it if things were quiet around here?"). In those twenty minutes, Michael drops both minute-by-minute time and continuity entirely. In the middle of a take, he lets the camera fall, with what looks like arbitrary abandon, into some object or stretch of color and lets it rest there, insistently, for too long; that is, until the viewer's

ability to watch it comfortably elapses and it has become
meaningless as an image. The urgency of boredom is enforced by the knowledge that, all this time, things are happening to Celia, and we're not seeing all of it. She's changing her
clothes, finding the bus station, being stopped by Terry's policeman father (Mark Pauley). But our ability to follow her,
the connection that lets us invade her privacy, is now faltering
and discontinuous, and so we find Manny Farber writing that
Michael has "pumped the movie full of manufactured space,
trying to liberate the Rice character into a life that continues
when the movie is over . . . he wants to show us that he appreciates the transciency of his vision." These processes are
familiar devices in *Adult Mail* (the changing of the deposi-
tions from scene to scene) and *Rotogravure,* both done in
1968, but are then applied only transitionally in *Scaled Down*
(1969) and *Positron* (1972).

Since *Governments* Michael has had a consistent crew and
acting company, enough of whom can get free for a few
months at any given time so that he can always start production on short notice. This way it's possible for each film to take
place in a city where a major political or social crisis is under-
way: the drug scandal and sabotage of construction by the
students in *Cloud Chamber,* the newspaper strike in *Government,* the pornography trial which is in the forefront of
Adult Mail, and so on. There are several uses of this motif
beyond the obvious effect of guaranteeing the inclusion of political material. For one thing, an attempt is made as work on
the production progresses to work the dispute into the plot as
much as possible, to give the characters affiliations on one
side or another, even to have the actors pursue these affiliations off-camera when possible. Thus Michael insures that the
true story is mated with his outline, such that the characters
will be responsible to unpredictable events beyond his control.
What is most striking about this is to see the actors involved,
on film, with people who aren't playing parts at all.

When Michael has a partial script completed (usually written by himself in collaboration with Spiegel or Ted Blau), he begins watching the papers for an accessible city where there is trouble he can use. Once his decision is made, he can get the full company and a van full of equipment to the location within three days. There they rent a house they can live in for the duration of the production, and afterward Michael takes the film back to Sacramento for synching and editing.

On the first night in town, when everyone else has begun moving in, Michael goes to whatever bar or restaurant is said to be a hangout for one faction in the dispute. He picks a table or space from which he can see as much of the room as possible, then starts circulating and attracting as many people as he can back to his position. He buys drinks and food. Every night he comes back, treating people and making friends, playing down the film as a project, just asking if he can take some pictures at what is expected to be an important meeting or confrontation. Then he goes to the other side's place and does the same thing. He finds it useful to offer cigarettes. He buys a pack of unfiltered kings, a pack of filters, a pack of menthol filters. Smiling, he opens a pack one-handed without looking, his eyes on the door of a bar or a MacDonald's, his thumb pulling the red tearstrip across the top of the cellophane wrapper as he watches for faces, reconstructing the clippings in his mind.

The probable reason that I lose parts of the films is that I never really see them to begin with. What happens is that the timing of the light's variations provides a way out, to places I don't remember. To locations: a dim stately bar where cold glasses leave perfect water rings on the hand-rubbed oak; a beautiful street in the financial district of an old European city where I walk, alone, after dark; empty spotless train stations where my only choice is to wait. The silence in the movies is layered so carefully as to provide a cover; I learn to fall forward again after years of steadying myself. It's not like being stupefied by Jimmy's songs when they were on the radio and it's not like traveling by signal. Equations don't work. But the surroundings, including the screen in front of me, fold up, and I go in slowly, brushing other lives, my head down, my hands wrapped together under my chin.

They smuggled me my mail: *Gourmet, Artforum, Business Week, Vintage,* Neiman-Marcus, Hammacher-Schlemmer, Pfaelzer Brothers, Harry and David, Greenland Studios, the Wisconsin Cheese Man, Sunset House, and our house organ, *TTW On-the-Grow-Notes,* published the same day the *Time* article came out. I looked at the *Notes* for news of myself.

Michael warns that when you mention a splice to most people, they think of the tic of light and missed syllable in a bad print, not realizing that splicing is any joining of two pieces of film, and as such is the basic method of editing and composing a finished print. Furthermore, an expert editor can splice one sequence to another with no suggestion that an omission has occurred. When he wants to drop a line of dialogue, he connects what come before to what comes after and when the film is screened, the line in question never existed. So the general supposition is that this technique lowers the "stakes" of filmmaking by lessening the number of variables and giving the editor the power to regulate the action even after the fact.

But Michael reminds us that the opposite is true: splicing *increases* the stakes, because the unadvised exclusion of a breath or gesture that belongs in the film will disturb everyone in the audience because they know exactly what belongs there, whether they know this consciously or not. They know better than the director, and as of that omission he has lost them.

Michael was in his room on the first floor behind the kitchen, putting away *Cloud Chamber,* which he had been showing me half an hour before. It was the only white room in the house. A wire ran overhead with strips of 35-millimeter film clipped to it. On the desk were a typewriter and an enlarger and a lot of papers, and on the opposite wall was an old porcelain sink.

"Hello?" he said when I came in.

"I want to see that again," I said. "I missed some."

But he continued putting it away. "So now you know you're out," he said. "Now that you've read it, you believe it. Without a trace." He shook his head. "What do you suppose they'll use that space for? Someone who has no idea what he's doing, right?"

He turned off his floor lamp, a household bulb set in the kind of conical silver fixture used for movie lighting. Now the only light in the room was from a small desk lamp, and the shadows of his fingers were long on the wall as he put the three reels in their box.

"You peeked," I said, sitting down on the bed.

He shrugged, then went to a shelf over the sink and took down his Pentax. He flattened his back against the wall opposite me, took a step forward, knelt, and began taking pictures.

"Won't it be too dark?" I said.

THREE

"I hear you singing in the wires."
　　　　—JIMMY WEBB, "Wichita Lineman"

Very soon now, any month, information will start disappearing from the memory banks of all the computers in the world. This won't be a matter of anyone deliberately tapping or erasing the material. It will find its own way out. It is possible for holes in cards to heal, for leads to lead nowhere, for magnetic particles positioned on tape to align themselves with silence. Those data never wanted in to begin with, and now, all by themselves, they are going to desert. By the process of elimination, the same few names will come up again and again, every day a smaller variety of names printing out with greater frequency of repetition until finally there are no more names available. I have all this legal pressure on me, or I could give you the names of people who know what's going to happen and are getting out of the business already.

I had my first inkling of this in a conversation with Michael on the first morning after I told him we could go ahead with shooting. I'd gone out in Steve's car and gotten us some doughnuts at a shop on the mall, and now Michael was saying that it would make more sense to pick a new target for action by signals, and to follow that progress in the film, than to re-stage the action I had already run in LA.

"You know what's computerized now?" he asked me.

"What?"

"All the draft stuff," he said.

"Including local?"

He nodded. "The Sacramento board just got it last year. Pat's action group had this girl who was clerking in there un-dercover and she was ripping off a few cards every week to see if that would throw it off, just taking five or six out at ran-dom."

"Stealing the cards wouldn't make any difference," I said, "there's an override that goes back and duplicates the infor-mation if the remaining cards are in sequence. I worked on it. What did she do with them?"

"What, the cards? I don't know," said Michael. "But you could do the same thing to the draft computer that you did to the others, mess it up so everybody comes out ineligible or something. And then we could make the movie around that, just have you—"

"Aren't all those records duplicated somewhere, though?"

He thought a minute, spreading a dust of confectioner's sugar on the tabletop, then said, "Well, in order to do the movie with you really doing it, you have to make the equip-ment again and make up the programs and everything, right? So then the movie shows how it's done, and we start screen-ings in the fall—I mean, this is still a movie, it's not just a training film or anything, but we show basically how it's done and then all of a sudden next winter you have all these people building their own equipment and going into their own boards and then Rand and Dow and all those—"

"It'll take a couple of weeks to make the equipment," I said.

"I want that time for preproduction anyway, and we have to order some new cameras and lights. A lot of my stuff doesn't even work now."

"Okay," I said, "are there people who can steal us some printouts and things?"

What's amazing, looking back on this—watching for behavior here—is that I wasn't thinking about the politics at all. The politics became the pretext, retroactively, for what I'd done, including the embezzling, but not until the trial got under way in LA, and by that time there was the June 20 Committee (the day I got arrested). All these people say that the movie project was a wet dream on Michael's part and a bitter gesture on mine because of being ignored in *Notes,* but all I could think of then was the idea of having so many strangers working from my instructions, a new kind of technician who—with Michael's help—would appreciate fully the implications of what they were doing when they worked with frequencies. That was all I wanted. It was during that conversation that I got excited for the first time about making all the computers go dumb, and the film seemed like the first step. It's taken us seven years to realize that it works best when no one pushes, that the tendency of languages is to unwrite themselves, that codes will go for their yellow capsules rather than be broken. But I got very optimistic then and told Michael everything I was thinking. In return he took some notes in his spiral notebook, nodding, tapping the table, taking the flow of material like a telegraph terminal. When I was done he put the notebook away and, looking straight at me, said, "That's really plausible," and then we began to plot the movie.

Midday in a rundown part of Sacramento. Vacco (myself) enters a phone booth at a gas station and makes two calls, his voice lost to us through the glass. When he's finished he runs across the street to a weathered Mustang with a young man at the wheel. Vacco gets in. They drive away quickly but not recklessly. There are no other people in the sequence, which consists of about ten takes: we pan into the booth with Vacco and stop as he shuts the door. The calls are covered by two alternating medium shots, one low-angle, one head-on, with a long establishing shot of the block inserted while he's dialing the second one. Then there's another long shot for his exit from the booth and the run across the street—same scope as the establishing shot but from the opposite angle—followed by an insert of Vacco's hand on the car door, a high-angle medium of him getting in and sitting down, tracking forward a foot for his short conversation with the driver (again, inaudible; the only sound on the track is wind and a truck offscreen), switching over to a medium shot of Vacco from over the driver's shoulder as the car starts pulling away from the curb, and then back to the long shot as the car gets two blocks away from us and starts to turn right onto a cross street. It's black and white, with good focus, too much grain, and nice steady dollying and panning. The new equipment made a big difference, even to the point of smoothing out the shooting style. The only hand-held shot is the one taken from over Steve's shoulder, a shot which boxes my face into a triangle formed by the corner of his window and the line of his jacket from his neck to the point of his shoulder. There's just an instant of camera jiggle, where my head, a bald ball at three-quarters to the camera, freefloats in the dark of the car, then regains its equilibrium, the up-and-down motion settling out to an intangible level by the last second of the take.

That was the only part of the planned movie that ever got shot. I took the cards and printouts from the girl who met me at the bar so I could look them over, but the bar was too dark so she said she'd steal some more and we'd get that part another day.

In the rest of Michael's outline, Vacco goes from the phone booth to a bar and meets a Student Mobe girl who gives him stolen cards and printouts from the draft board. He opens an active file on the language and hardware being used. In an interview, he explains which books and journals to read for information on programming languages and how to design programs that will introduce crippling discrepancies into any standing program, and how to feed those programs to computers over any telephone. I was worried about this last part because it's so much talk and I was afraid it would drag, but Michael was going to intercut portions of his Chicago footage, which was very good, by the way.

At an electronics hobby shop in the Sacramento suburbs, Vacco buys all the necessary parts for his frequency-making equipment. We see him assembling the box and compiling charts that match the draft-board computer's programming language with tables of frequencies. Later he sits in an armchair, playing beeps from the box into a home telephone as he reads from a list of numbers titled "June birthdays—flat feet."

Everything on the film was to have been real, including that last sequence. Our intention was expertise, which is why we spent almost every minute of the two preproduction weeks together, talking to almost nobody else and teaching each other all the craft we could before shooting started. It was no accident that Michael was in my room, with a camera, when the arresting FBI agent came to the house a few days after we shot the phone booth stuff.

So Jimmy stopped writing big hits. Very soon after the arrest, a matter of a few months, his share of airplay dropped as quickly as it had risen and hasn't changed much since.

I've never believed the story about the Student Mobe girl being an informer, nor do I think it really matters. If anything, it's my fault for not recognizing how much power can go into a small space, like three minutes of music. The trick is that with information you need the construction and combination of symbols, which gives you that misleading multiplicity again, but power is a single sustained tone with nothing to say. You can get a lot of it in a small place. At the time of Jimmy's hits, several of us were on orders every minute. It didn't feel that different from normal life, but then Jimmy's technique was sophisticated and had distance as a cover, so it could be forever before we pin it down.

What worries me is that he must think I'm angry for the way he singled me out. I'd like to tell him that I understand, that I'm not mad, but they won't even let me talk to him on the phone. The last time I called up they said he was working on a new solo album. I have that one. All it is is music, like everything else he's done since that summer. I don't know if anyone's done the actual research yet of digging out the lyrics and melodies from during and after that period, I mean complete copies of both sets, but that would be an interesting project for someone and probably not too unwieldy.

Anyway he's stopped, so it's one of two things: either the connection left him or he decided he'd gotten what he needed and it would be safest if he played it quiet for a while, and if he was turning things back over to me there was no need to have the waves coming off the radio anymore. The third possibility, of Jimmy running up against the program that incurs silence, wide silence, silence in the balance of matter, is also worth considering, and there's the chance that after he got cocky he got scared. Certainly, the blatancy of the clues he was dropping at one time is amazing: all the lyrics to "Wichita Lineman," the one about the folk technician who is "searching in the sun for another overload," but especially the arrangement (which one of the newsmagazines called "the wow-wow-wow sound of wind whipping through the wires" but which is in fact the completely wireless heartbeat of freefloating control waves). It's clear, looking back to that summer, that I got the pictures of him at work for a reason: they were feedback. Every transmission has two ends. I can understand his reason for keeping low profile now. It's ridiculous to ask him to share his findings when he's already pointed the way to so much, and it's important to understand that for someone in his position the situation is getting harder, not easier. It was during the last part of the trial that "Galveston," which is "about" a Texas boy in Vietnam but actually is concerned with this feedback phenomenon (*"I can see her standing by the water . . ."*) got hot. It was the instrumental tag, the music with nothing said alongside it, that stung the hardest. I should have known exactly what was happening the first time I heard it—out on bail, going to lunch in Marv Loewinson's car—and started crying.

So when will the real facts become known, if ever? Should the main signal be closed off, who will know how to get from one step to the next? How will we know it's happening? What are the five danger signs of dematerialization? How do we prepare? How do we prevent? How do we get back the power we must have had once, and need now, to screen in advance everything that goes on the radio, everything that passes a tape head, everything that is said to us everywhere we go? What happens if we know everything we need to know and still, in the most crucial of instants, our concentration slips and leaves us staring at what we were never supposed to see?

There's still this difficulty with written accounts, the real sensations peeling off and fluttering away, the specifics invoked just to make encouraging noise. So let me close with the film of the arrest. The film per se is only fifteen seconds long, but I had Michael freeze a frame in the middle, a process whereby you print one frame over and over so that it appears that the projector has stopped. After the door opens and I walk toward it, as the man in the suit comes in and reaches into his pocket for the little billfold with the badge in it, there's one image you'll see for a long time, almost a minute. It's me and the cop—his front, my back—both of us from the waist up, each getting half the frame, a moderately low angle so that we find ourselves looking up into his face. We're drawn there anyway by that diagonal composition with the chair behind me and my arm coming up. Look at his eyes. I know there's a lot of grain and a slight softening of line due to camera movement, which is why I asked Michael to stretch it out. Look carefully at the cop's face as he brings his head up, the skin stretching a little against his jaw, his mouth bunching as he starts to talk. I wish we had sound on this, because there's a slight crack in his voice, but anyway: the eyes. There's an expression of fear, which is to be expected be-

08

cause, let's face it, taking orders when you don't know where they're coming from is at once the easiest and the most exacting kind of obedience, for me or him or the girl or whoever. If you look closely at the right eye, the one on our left, there's the tiniest streak of moisture coming out of the corner and sliding about halfway down the side of his nose. Look very carefully because this is the last information we get. Soon the action starts again and he turns his head away and that's it. Can everybody see?